THE GHOSTS OF TREBLINKA

THE GHOSTS OF TREBLINKA

Scott M. Baker

Also by Scott M. Baker

Rotter Nation
Rotter Apocalypse
Yeitso

Novellas
Nazi Ghouls From Space
Twilight of the Living Dead
This Is Why We Can't Have Nice Things During the Zombie Apocalypse
Dead Water

Anthologies
Cruise of the Living Dead and Other Stories
Incident on Ironstone Lane and Other Horror Stories
Crossroads in the Dark V: Beyond the Borders
Rejected for Content
Roots of a Beating Heart
The Zombie Road Fan Fiction Collection
The Collector
Vlada: Tales of the Damned
Through the Aftermath: A Post-Apocalyptic Anthology

A Schattenseite Book

The Ghosts of Treblinka
by Scott M. Baker.
Copyright © 2024. All Rights Reserved.
Print Edition
ISBN-13: 979-8-9884973-4-9

Cover Art © Warren Design

This book is dedicated to the twelve million innocent souls slaughtered during the Holocaust: Jews, Gypsies, homosexuals, the mentally disabled, socialists, Freemasons, anyone who openly opposed National Socialism, and the thousands of other innocent people throughout occupied Europe.

A Warning to My Readers

The Ghosts of Treblinka is not intended to exploit the tragedy of the Holocaust for the sake of selling books. Quite the opposite. By writing this novel, I hope to make people aware of the horrors that took place throughout Europe between 1933 and 1945 due to the Third Reich. As with *The Ghosts of Salem Village* and *The Ghosts of Bethlehem Asylum*, the flashback sequences are meant to make people aware of the extent of the inhumanity and suffering inflicted on the innocent victims of one of the darkest moments in history. Although the characters of those at Treblinka are fictional, the nightmares they endured are based on the accounts of the handful of survivors who survived.

The flashback sequences in this book are extremely disturbing, even more so because such atrocities occurred daily. Over nine hundred thousand people were exterminated at Treblinka, one of four death camps set up by the SS for the sole purpose of genocide. I strongly urge you to read that chapter to realize the extent of man's inhumanity during the Holocaust.

CHAPTER ONE

Prostyn, Poland

"HOW MUCH FURTHER?" asked Jochen from the back seat of the Volkswagen Golf, his voice quivering with apprehension.

"Calm down." Werner glanced at his friend in the rearview mirror.

"We've been on the road for hours."

"We'll be there soon."

Hans shifted in the passenger seat to look at Jochen. "Just make sure your phone is charged. We've driven too far to make this video to turn back because you forgot to plug it in."

"It is." Jochen held up the cell phone and shook it to show the charger chord was plugged in. "But do you think it's a good idea to post this?"

"Are you wimping out on us?"

"No." Jochen blurted his answer, which only added to his nervousness.

Hans chuckled and glanced over at Werner. "I told you we should have left him behind. He ain't nothing but a pussy."

"I am not."

"I am not," Hans mimicked Jochen in an effeminate voice.

"Screw you." Jochen punched the back of Hans' chair.

"Knock it off," snapped Werner. "Both of you. I didn't drive all the way from Munich to have you two screw this up."

An uneasy silence fell over the car.

Werner had been planning this for weeks. He had been a YouTube influencer for a while, promoting the National

Socialist agenda and trying to convince the mindless masses that the problems facing the world could be traced back to one source – the Jews. His podcasts were well-received by his fanbase. However, despite doing three weekly programs for the past two years, his viewership never climbed above ten thousand viewers. That would change after tonight.

The conflict between Israel and Hamas offered the perfect opportunity to change that. Popular opinion shifted overnight against the Jews, providing the perfect opportunity to push home his ideology and show the people that Hitler had been right all along. What better place to do it than one of the locations that had achieved so much toward the goal? Werner had been planning this for weeks, fine-tuning his script and figuring out which camera angles would be the most effective. Tonight would hopefully wake up the masses to what they faced and prompt them into action.

Werner continued driving until he reached the town of Treblinka, then turned onto the main road leading southeast. After a few miles, the sign he had been searching for appeared on the shoulder:

Niemiecki nazistowski obóz zagłady i obóz pracy 1941 – 1944
The Nazi German Extermination and Labor Camp
1941 – 1944

He motioned toward it. "We're here."

Werner slowed and scanned the area, making certain no one was around to see them enter, then turned onto the driveway. Once in the parking lot, he pulled the car against some trees to keep it out of sight, shut down the engine, and climbed out. His friends met him around back. Werner popped open the trunk and removed three backpacks and three flashlights, handing one to each of them.

"We've discussed the plan several times, so no need to go over it. We go in, do what we have to, and get out of here as quickly as possible. Jochen, use the burner phone. You'll upload the video on the way home and then dispose of it."

Without saying another word, he switched on his flashlight and headed for their destination.

Exiting the parking lot, the three turned left and followed a pathway through the woods for several minutes. The quiet was unsettling. They were far enough away from the nearest town that the only sounds came from a chorus of crickets broken intermittently by the hoot of a barn owl, the howl of a wolf, or Jochen's nervous breathing. They eventually emerged into a clearing fifty feet wide that stretched for half a mile. After a few hundred feet, the flashlight beams fell upon a series of cement blocks similar in appearance to railroad ties that emerged from the woods to their right, hugged the tree line for several yards, and then branched off into the center of the clearing. Werner followed the blocks until they reached a slightly elevated platform paralleling the blocks. Ascending the platform, he followed a stone path leading into another large clearing surrounded by trees.

Jochen shrugged his shoulders as a cold chill ran down his spine. "This place gives me the creeps."

"Grow a pair," snapped Werner. "We're almost there."

Hans exited the stone path and walked over to a chunk of marble with a polished façade on the grass. Placing his backpack on the ground, he opened it, removed a can of white spray paint, and shook it several times before painting a swastika on the surface.

Werner sighed in frustration. "Knock that off and get over here."

"I thought we came here to vandalize the place?"

"We did. But I want to get the video first."

Hans tossed the paint can into his backpack and followed his friends up the stone path.

The flashlight beams fell upon a monolith in the center of the clearing composed of scores of massive granite blocks.

Those overhanging the top had designs carved into them. Werner raised the beam to see them better. Two hands at the top center of the monolith raised their palms skyward as if calling to God. Carvings of human skulls surrounded the hands.

"There it is." Werner unslung his backpack. He removed a can of spray, which he shook, and then handed his cell phone to Jochen. "Get ready to record."

Jochen stared at the screen. "What's your passcode?"

"0420."

Jochen accessed the phone and called up the video camera. Werner and Hans donned their outfits: a pair of black masks emblazoned with white SS runes that covered the bottom half of their faces, black knitted ski hats with the words *Heil Hitler* sown into the fabric, and red Nazi armbands with a black swastika emblazoned inside a white circle. With their identities hidden but their politics bared to everyone, they positioned themselves in front of the monolith.

"We're ready," said Werner.

Jochen raised the cell phone and pressed the record button. The light from the phone illuminated the two teenagers. They held their flashlights vertically to shine on their faces.

"We're here at Treblinka," began Werner. "The Jews set up this memorial in remembrance of the lives lost here during World War II. We're here today to honor the service of those SS officers who struggled to make Europe *Juden frei*. Those of us who know the truth see this as a testament to Hitler's grand idea of ridding the world of the ethnic decay caused by these parasites. The Nazi defeat only doomed the world to decades of unrest with the communist takeover of East Europe and the establishment of the pariah state of Israel. The Jewish communists are still working to destroy the world's economy, and the Zionist occupation of Palestine has created nothing but war in the Middle East. Wake up, people! Don't believe the propaganda perpetrated by the Jewish socialist media. These vermin are succeeding in their goal of world domination. It's patriots like us, people who still believe in the righteousness of our cause, who are the only thing preventing Jewish control of the world. Join us to make the entire world *Juden frei*. Long live National Socialism and the memory of our *Fuhrer*! From the river to the sea!"

Werner and Hans snapped to attention, extending their right arms at a forty-five-degree angle.

"Sieg heil! Sieg heil! Sieg heil!"

Their verbal tirade finished, both teenagers removed paint cans from their backpacks and painted half a dozen swastikas on the monolith's surface. When done, they tossed the cans aside. Werner turned back to the camera.

"This is what we think of this disgusting monument honoring those who are destroying mankind."

Werner and Hans spun around, lodged the flashlights under their shoulders, unzipped their trousers, and urinated on the monolith. They zipped up and turned back to the camera.

"This place should be a testimony to those who fought for the right—"

Werner dropped his flashlight and stumbled back against the monolith, gasping for air. Hans fell to his knees, choking.

"What's wrong?" asked Jochen, still filming.

Werner turned to the camera and gasped. "Help me."

Jochen ran over to his friends. He laid the cell phone against one of the backpacks so it filmed what was going on, then placed his ear against Werner's chest. His heart still beat, though pounding dangerously fast.

"Are you having a heart attack?"

Werner shook his head and struggled to talk. "Can't... breathe."

Jochen lifted Werner onto his feet, spun him around, and performed the Heimlich maneuver. Nothing dislodged.

One of the discarded flashlight beams illuminated Hans, whose face had turned blue. The teenager leaned forward, struggling for air. Dropping to his knees, Hans clasped his hands, placed them under his ribcage, and tried to clear his windpipe, but with no results. After several minutes, his body went limp and slumped to the ground.

Jochen tried the Heimlich maneuver on Werner a second time. The teenager broke free from his friend's embrace, collapsed, and pounded his chest. His face had also turned blue.

"Air," he gasped, then went limp, lying lifeless beside Hans.

Jochen panicked. His friends were dead. He could not leave them here. The authorities would find the bodies, identify them, and trace him as part of the group, which would drop him into a world of shit. Yet he would never be able to drag both corpses back to the car.

He reached into Werner's pocket and searched for the keys. His only option was to get out of there and return to Munich. If he could make it home, his sister would cover for him, testifying he had been with her all—

Jochen stopped breathing. He inhaled deeply, but no oxygen entered his lungs. He tried to remain calm, hoping it was merely a panic attack after watching his friends die. That thought proved incorrect. No matter how hard Jochen tried, he could not catch his breath. Terror welled up inside him with each failed attempt to take in air. His heart pounded rapidly. He kept telling himself to relax and take deep breaths, but it did no good. His vision grew restricted, and he started to slip into unconsciousness. Jochen leaned against the monolith and slid down into a crouch.

A spectral image appeared in front of him, one more terrifying than his inability to breathe.

Jochen rasped out the words "I'm sorry" before death took his life.

CHAPTER TWO

One week later

TATYANA SAT AT her desk, typing away on her laptop as she worked on her dissertation. Nick watched television on the sofa, dressed in his 1940s naval dress uniform he was murdered in, keeping the volume turned down so it did not bother her. Nostradamus curled up beside Nick, snoring lightly.

Nick blurted out, "That bastard."

"What are you talking about?"

"Look at this." Nick turned up the television volume.

Joel stood in a studio decorated to look like a Tarot reading room. He did a slow walk through the set as he spoke.

"Welcome to the premiere episode of *Paranormal Explained*. I'm Joel Carbone. Tonight, we'll be delving into the most disturbing haunting since Amityville in 1975. I led a paranormal investigation of Bethlehem Asylum near Craig, Colorado, an institution with a dark past that rivals some of the most bizarre medical facilities in history. We conducted an overnight stay at the asylum."

As Joel talked, video clips of each participant the night of the incident flashed across the screen for three seconds with their name underneath. Tatyana was listed last.

"Each of us went in not knowing the nightmares we would face. Some of those who entered Bethlehem Asylum that night did not live long enough to see the dawn. This show is dedicated to them.

"Everything that was recorded during the investigation, including the deaths of my friends, has been included in this broadcast. Viewer discretion is advised. Having said that, get ready to watch our paranormal investigation of Bethlehem Asylum."

The show cut into a five-minute segment, narrated by Joel, of the history of the institution and the riot that occurred in March 1951. Following the introduction, it went into the meeting of the team, their arrival at the asylum, and the horrifying events that took place. The footage had been edited to exclude all of Joel's cowardly moments, and additional interview spots were added to make him appear as the team's hero. To his credit, Joel included the full footage of all the deaths and the final confrontation between Dr. Savage and the abused patients, though Tatyana knew that was done for ratings and not to pay homage to those who had lost their lives. When the show finished, Joel appeared back in the studio with a few wrap-up remarks before thanking the audience for joining him. The program ended with photos of those who had died that night, accompanied by the years of their births and deaths, and then the end credits rolled.

Nick shut off the television. "I can't believe the son of a bitch aired that show after what happened."

"I can."

"He made himself look like the hero of that night."

Tatyana shrugged. "He's the producer. He can do anything he wants."

The experience at Bethlehem Asylum had been so disturbing for Tatyana that she had not undertaken any investigations since, concentrating instead on finishing her doctorate, partially because she needed to complete it and partially as an excuse not to delve into the realm of the paranormal anymore. However, she missed the investigations. Being able to communicate with the afterlife was a gift, and she considered helping those spirits stuck in this realm a calling she could not avoid. However, after losing four colleagues during the last investigation, she was afraid to get involved again.

"You'll do another one when you're up to it," said Nick from the sofa.

"Do another what?"

"An investigation. It's in your blood."

"Are you reading my mind?" asked Tatyana accusingly.

"I don't have to. I know you too well. You feel this way after every difficult investigation. And each time, you agree to take on cases worse than the previous one." Nick leaned his head back so he could see her. "It's embedded in your nature."

Though Tatyana would not admit it, Nick was right. She knew that, eventually, she would return to conducting paranormal investigations.

Nick huffed from the sofa. "I should go haunt that asshole. What do you think?"

For a moment, Tatyana considered letting him do it. Joel deserved whatever happened to him. But she thought better about it. It wasn't like he would learn anything from the experience.

"Leave Joel alone. He's not—"

Tatyana's cell phone rang. She picked it up from the desk. The phone number was from an unknown caller with a 202 area code. She accepted it.

"Hello?"

"Is this Tatyana Reynolds?" The man on the other end spoke excellent English though with a heavy Eastern European accent.

"Who's calling?"

"I'm with the Polish Embassy in Washington, D.C. Ambassador Wojciechowski is on the other line. He wants to talk to you."

"About what?"

"About a situation we have here in our country."

"I'm no longer—" Before she could finish, elevator music came through the speakers. A few seconds later, another voice came on the line. Like the initial caller, his English was perfect but with an accent.

"This is Ambassador Wojciechowski. Am I speaking with Tatyana Reynolds?"

"You are. But as I tried to tell the other gentleman, I'm no longer engaged in paranormal investigations."

"Please hear me out before you say no."

Tatyana sighed to herself. "Go ahead."

"Thank you. I would not normally bother you, but my country faces an extremely sensitive situation that requires the services of an expert paranormal investigator."

"There are others more experienced and qualified than me."

"More experienced, yes. But they're all *szarlatan* who are out only to make a name for themselves."

"*Szarlatan?*"

"Sorry. It's how you say in English charlatan. We need someone who's reliable to resolve this issue for us."

"And someone not looking for fame who will publicly air this and embarrass you?" Tatyana immediately regretted her snarky response. "I'm sorry. That was uncalled for."

"No apology necessary. Your cynicism is understandable considering some of the cases you've been involved in. Please be assured, our desire is not to keep this from the public but to find peace for the tormented spirits."

"How many spirits are we talking about?"

A sigh came over the phone, not of frustration but sadness. "More than you can imagine."

The despondency in the ambassador's tone piqued her interest. "I'm intrigued."

Nick chuckled from the sofa. "I knew you'd get back in the game sooner or later."

Tatyana crumbled a piece of paper and threw it at him. The object passed through his spectral image and fell on the floor. Nostradamus dived off the couch, grabbed it in his mouth, and proceeded to tear it apart.

"So, you'll take the case?"

"Before I say yes, I'll need to know more. Is the cleansing in Poland or here in the States?"

"It's in Poland. But don't worry. We'll take care of all travel expenses."

"That's not what I'm concerned about. I enjoy traveling. What's the nature of the haunting?"

A slight hesitation came over the line. "I'd rather not say over an unsecured line."

"Is it that bad?"

"Sadly, yes. I can arrange to fly you down to Washington for a briefing or, if you prefer, have someone meet you in New Hampshire."

"If you don't mind, I'd prefer to meet here. I'm trying to finish my dissertation."

"Completely understandable. Would two o'clock tomorrow afternoon be agreeable?"

"That's perfect."

"Do you want to meet at your residence or someplace public?"

"My house is fine." Tatyana gave the ambassador the address.

"Thank you, Miss Reynolds."

"My pleasure. But there are no promises I'll take the case."

"I understand. But when you hear what we have to tell you, I hope you'll change your mind."

The conversation ended, and Tayana placed her cell phone back on the desk.

Nick chuckled. "You can take the girl out of the paranormal, but you can't take the paranormal out of the girl."

"I didn't say yes. Though I'll admit, I'm interested in what he has to say."

Nick shifted to face her. "Politicians have a way of doing that. They get your hopes up, shake your hand, kiss your baby—"

"I don't have children."

"—and once they're elected, they spend years lining their own pockets."

"That might have been the way things were done in the forties, but not today."

Nick narrowed his eyes. "Are you serious?"

"Yes. Today, they're much worse."

Nick laughed heartily. "I'll leave you alone so you can get your work done."

"You'll be back at two tomorrow, won't you?"

"I wouldn't miss this for anything."

Nick turned into a swirling mist for several seconds before disappearing with a poof. It usually aggravated Tatyana when Nick did that, but after being friends with him for so long, she had become used to his dramatic exits.

Nostradamus looked at her confusedly, still not used to Nick's way of departing.

"It's okay, boy. He'll be back."

Nostradamus left the torn remnants of the paper ball on the carpet, climbed on the sofa, and went back to sleep.

Tatyana returned to writing her dissertation, but after her conversation with the Polish ambassador, she found it difficult to concentrate on her work.

CHAPTER THREE

TATYANA SPENT THE morning working until one o'clock. Then she changed out of her usual work-at-home clothes—pajama bottoms, a Salem t-shirt, a house robe, and slippers—into casual business attire. When she exited the bedroom, Nick sat on the sofa watching television with Nostradamus curled up beside him. She had a pair of couch potatoes for roommates.

She had finished preparing a pot of coffee for her guests when the doorbell rang.

Nostradamus raised his head.

"It's okay, boy," said Tatyana as she crossed the living room. The dog jumped off the sofa and followed her to the door.

"Nick, shut off the TV."

"Your command is my wish."

When Tatyana opened the door, two men stood there, both dressed in expensive suits. The older of the two was in his mid-fifties, of average height and build, with greying hair and beard. He had a friendly yet confident demeanor about him. She guessed the younger of the two to be in his late twenties or early thirties. He stood six feet in height with blonde hair and piercing brown eyes, and seemed more professional than his compatriot.

"Are you Miss Reynolds?" asked the older gentleman.

"I am."

He smiled and offered his hand. "I'm Ambassador Wojciechowski. We talked yesterday on the phone."

Tatyana took the hand and gave it a firm pump. "It's a pleasure to meet you."

"This is Stanisław Półtorzycki of the CBSP."

"You can call me Stanisław." He offered his hand. "Thank you for agreeing to meet us."

"No problem. What is the CBSP?"

"The *Centralne Biuro Śledcze Policji*, or the Central Investigation Bureau of the Police. It's similar to your FBI." Stanisław broke into a smile and crouched. "And this must be Nostradamus. I've heard a lot about you."

The dog's tail wagged furiously. He stepped toward the two men for his mandatory ear scratch.

"Won't you gentlemen please come in?"

They did. Nostradamus stuck close to his new friends.

"Have a seat. I made coffee. Do you want some?"

"Thank you." The ambassador sat on the sofa along with Stanisław.

Tatyana exited the kitchen with three mugs of coffee on a tray. She placed it on the coffee table and slid into the recliner. Nostradamus curled up on the floor behind her. Nick took her spot behind the desk.

"You seem to know a lot about me." Tatyana poured three mugs, passed two to her guests, and grinned. "Are you spying on me?"

"Merely normal research." Stanisław scooped two spoonfuls of sugar into his coffee. "You have quite a reputation in the paranormal community."

"He means that in a positive way." The ambassador picked up his mug and blew on the coffee to cool it down.

"After the incident occurred and Warsaw decided we needed an expert in this field, I was assigned to find one we felt was reliable."

Tatyana took her mug and leaned back into the recliner. "Aren't there paranormal investigators in Poland?"

"Quite a few, actually. But none have the experience you

do." Stanisław sat forward and placed his mug on the coffee table. "We're more concerned with getting the best person for the job, not the most convenient. Your name had one of the highest search results on Google, so I checked you out further. Salem and Miami Cruise Lines both hired your services, which is impressive, and I found no negative reviews of you. That makes you the perfect candidate to investigate this incident."

"That's the second time you've used the word incident. Can you tell me more?"

Stanisław reached behind him for the manila envelope he had brought. "Before I pass this to you, I need your assurance that you won't discuss its contents if you decide not to take the case."

"Do you need me to sign a non-disclosure agreement?"

"Your word is good enough for us."

"Thank you." Tatyana reached out for the envelope. "May I?"

Stanisław handed it to her. "Do you know what Treblinka is?"

"Wasn't that one of the concentration camps the Nazis set up in Poland?"

The ambassador jumped in. "Actually, it was a death camp."

"What's the difference?"

"A concentration camp also served as a labor camp. When the trains arrived, those prisoners who were deemed fit enough to work were separated and consigned to slave labor. The rest went to the gas chamber. Everyone who arrived at a death camp was killed within the first few hours."

"Treblinka was the worst of the death camps," added Stanisław. "It was only in existence for fifteen months, but in that time, the Germans exterminated over nine hundred thousand men, women, and children, most of them Jews."

A wave of nausea welled up inside Tatyana at the thought of so many innocent people being butchered.

"The Germans destroyed Treblinka in 1944," continued Stanisław. "Leveled it. We only know about it today because a handful of prisoners who survived talked about it after the war. Today, it's one of many memorials to those slaughtered during the Holocaust."

Tatyana shook her head. "I can't even imagine the torment the spirits trapped there must be going through."

"It's intense," agreed the ambassador. "We've had numerous reports over the years from mediums, psychics, and people attuned to the spirit world of intense activity at Treblinka. Several years ago, one incident occurred where a woman was so overwhelmed, she had to be taken to a local hospital."

"Where do I come in?"

Stanisław removed a cell phone from his pocket and accessed it as he talked. "The incident we're referring to occurred ten days ago, and we're unable to explain. Three neo-Nazi podcasters were at Treblinka filming their vandalization of the memorials. They planned to air it later but never got the chance."

He handed the cell phone to Tatyana. "Press play."

She watched the video, disgusted by the level of anti-Semitism that still existed in the world. What attracted her attention were the last few minutes when the three bigots choked to death.

"What happened to them?"

"We're not sure." Stanisław motioned toward the envelope. "According to the autopsy reports, they died of asphyxiation."

"From what?" She opened the envelope and removed a translated version of the autopsy report and photographs of the victims at the scene and their autopsy photos.

"That's what baffled the coroner. There were no foreign substances in their lungs. No obstructions in their airways. No signs of strangulation. As you can see from the video, they just stopped breathing."

Tatyana studied the photos. "What's that structure behind

them?"

Stanisław glanced over at the ambassador and then back to Tatyana. "That was the location of the camp's gas chamber."

"Shit," mumbled Nick.

"You think they were suffocated by the spirits?"

"We have no other explanation. That's why we came to you."

"You want me to cleanse Treblinka? You realize how difficult that'll be?"

"I do. We're hoping you can at least... how do you say it? Placate the spirits."

"Placate them?"

"Calm them down might be a better phrase," said the ambassador.

Stanisław continued. "Our concern is if further such incidents occur. Treblinka is a monument to those who died during the Holocaust. We don't want to scare away any visitors who come to pay their respects. Or worse, attract more neo-Nazis who want to avenge their friends' deaths. We are trying to avoid a media circus. It needs to remain a site of solemnity and respect. That's why we came to you."

"We're willing to compensate you well if you accept." The ambassador removed a folded set of papers from his pocket and placed them on the coffee table. "One hundred thousand dollars plus expenses. We'll even arrange your transportation and hotel reservations. Can we count on you?"

Nick cleared his throat and shook his head, mouthing the word "No."

Tatyana read through the paperwork. Everything was simple. The contract did not even include a non-disclosure agreement.

"Is everything acceptable?" asked the ambassador.

"It is."

The ambassador's demeanor relaxed. He removed a pen from his jacket pocket and handed it to Tatyana. Out of the corner of her eye, she noticed Nick giving her a disapproving look. She signed both contracts and passed back one copy and the pen.

"Thank you."

"When do you need me?" asked Tatyana.

"As soon as possible," said the ambassador, obviously relieved.

"I'll need two days to get ready. And I'll also need to take Nostradamus with me. He detects spirits before I do."

"That can be arranged. Do you need us to provide anything?"

"No, thank you. I'll bring what I need with me."

The ambassador stood. "You have no idea how much my government appreciates this. My country owes you a debt of gratitude."

"It's my pleasure." Tatyana stood and offered her hand.

He shook it. "Stanisław will be accompanying you, if you don't mind."

"It'll be good to have an escort."

"Thanks," said Stanisław. "I'll call you once all the flight arrangements have been made."

Tatyana escorted the two men to the door, and they said their goodbyes.

As she came back into the living room, Nick stood. "I think you've gotten in way over your head."

"It can't be any worse than Bethlehem Asylum."

"Don't kid yourself. During the war, my brother was with the 9th Armored Infantry Battalion in Europe. His unit liberated the Buchenwald concentration camp. He wrote me a letter about what he witnessed. The horrors that went on in those camps were beyond imagination."

"If I can free these spirits, I'm doing a good thing. So, what's the problem?"

"You're going to experience unimaginable suffering, far greater than anything you've encountered before. I hope you can handle it."

Tatyana had not considered that possibility. Coming from Nick, who had experienced combat, the warning left her with an uneasy feeling.

"I hope you'll still accompany me."

"Of course I will. Just prepare yourself. The next few days are going to be an emotional nightmare."

"I appreciate your concern, but I'll be fine."

"I hope so. In any case, I'll be there for you. I'll leave you alone so you can return to work. See you in two days."

Nick's spectral image faded until it disappeared, foregoing his usual dramatic exit. The fact that this bothered Nick so much made her uncomfortable. Nothing ever upset him.

Tatyana pushed those thoughts aside and returned to working on her dissertation, hoping to complete the first draft before leaving for Poland.

CHAPTER FOUR

TATYANA RECLINED HER seat several inches, crossed her legs, and relaxed. Lifting her glass of burgundy off the central console tray, she swirled it around for a few seconds as if at a fancy wine tasting, then drank the remainder. Settling into the chair, she closed her eyes and rested. This was the first time Tatyana had flown business class, and she intended to enjoy every minute.

The Polish Embassy had arranged a direct flight from New York City to Warsaw via LOT Polish Airlines and purchased three seats: one for Tatyana, one for Nostradamus, and one for Stanisław, who would accompany her to Treblinka. The dog had curled up in the seat next to the window and had been asleep since shortly after takeoff. Stanisław occupied the seat across the aisle, thumbing through the paperwork in his briefcase. Tatyana attempted to get some sleep during the nine-hour flight.

Unfortunately, relaxation was the last thing she would get on this trip. The minute she closed her eyes, her mind focused on the nightmare that had been Poland's most notorious death camp.

Last night, she had gotten about an hour into her dissertation when curiosity overtook her, and she put it aside to read up on Treblinka. Finding information on the death camp was much easier than on the *Maria Doria* or Bethlehem Asylum. Typing the name in the Google search bar returned thousands of results.

After failing to solve the Jewish issue in Europe through

emigration and deportation, in January 1942, the Nazis settled on the Final Solution—extermination. As the ambassador had relayed earlier, concentration camps like Auschwitz divided their attention between murder and slave labor, which slowed the process. To expedite the murder of the Jews, the *Schutzstaffel*, more commonly known as the SS, the organization responsible for carrying out Hitler's genocidal wish, established four camps in Poland in 1943 solely dedicated to killing: Treblinka, Sobibor, Belzec, and Majdanek. Of the four, Treblinka was the smallest, taking up less than forty acres, yet it murdered the most civilians, anywhere between nine hundred thousand and one million, depending on the source. The only people who survived beyond the first two hours were those able-bodied men who were removed from the line to perform camp duties such as ransacking the victims' personal belongings or emptying the gas chamber and disposing of the remains. Once these individuals were no longer of use, they were filtered into the death procession. During its nightmarish existence of just over a year, the death camp received two trains of victims a day, six days a week, an average of more than fourteen thousand people daily. Only eighty-six Jews survived the ordeal, survivors of a mass breakout in August of 1943. Had it not been for them, the world would never have known of the horrors that took place at Treblinka.

What she found most disturbing was that Treblinka used primitive methods of extermination and disposal. While the other three death camps and the concentration camps murdered their victims with Zyklon B, a mixture composed primarily of hydrogen cyanide that suffocated those exposed to it within two minutes, Treblinka used carbon monoxide from the engine of a discarded Soviet tank to fill the gas chamber, a process that took more than ten minutes to kill its victims. While the other camps had specially made crematoriums to dispose of the remains, the final desecration for the deceased at Treblinka was to be buried in open pits.

As the Red Army closed in on the camp, the Nazis closed Treblinka. The remaining Jewish laborers were killed, the carcasses were dug up and burned in fire pits, the buildings were razed, and the area bulldozed to eliminate any indication of its existence. When the Nazis retreated, they left only forty acres of open field with a farmhouse constructed on the foundation of the SS bakery and built with bricks from the torn-down gas chamber. For years, no one knew the death camp existed until the war crimes trials were held after the war and the survivors came forward.

Tatyana began to think Nick was right, and she may have gotten in over her head on this one.

A hand gently touched her arm. "Are you asleep?"

Tatyana opened her eyes. Stanisław leaned across the aisle. "No. Just resting."

"Ambassador Wojciechowski texted me. A CBSP official will meet us at the gate so we can bypass Customs and Immigration. They've arranged for a car to take us to the hotel. We'll spend the night in Warsaw and head to Treblinka in the morning."

"Good. I can use some sleep." She paused before asking, "Have you ever been to Treblinka?"

"I'm ashamed to admit I've never visited any of the camps."

"Why are you ashamed of that?"

"The Holocaust is an unfortunate part of Polish history, and I should have gone to pay my respects. I was born after Communism collapsed. I'm of the generation that doesn't dwell on the past but looks to the future. Probably naïve on my part."

"Not naivety." Tatyana sighed. "It's a part of history we rarely discuss, even in the States. Most schools, if they even talk about it at all, only mention that six million Jews were killed."

"Rarely mentioned are the other six million who were also slaughtered. Slavs, socialists, Russian POWs, Catholics, Freemasons, homosexuals, the mentally disabled, and Gypsies.

The Nazis hated Gypsies as much as they did the Jews. As a percentage of their population, the Gypsies suffered greater losses than the Jews." Stanisław shook his head. "I guess this will be a learning experience for both of us."

Stanisław went back to reading material from his briefcase. Tatyana laid her head back, chuckling to herself as Nostradamus snored. She wished she could fall asleep as easily. But that would be impossible with everything running through her mind. Tatyana regretted not bringing along a book to distract her.

CHAPTER FIVE

THE CBSP HAD booked Tatyana into the Warsaw Marriott Hotel, which was luxurious. Her room had two double beds, one of which Nostradamus immediately claimed as his. Tatyana showered and then called room service, ordering a chicken Caesar salad and a bottle of Burgundy. The salad satiated her appetite. The wine relaxed her enough to fall asleep early.

At eight o'clock in the morning, Tatyana and Nostradamus went down to the lobby. Stanisław waited by the reception desk. Upon seeing her, he came over and smiled.

"Good morning. I hope you had a good night's sleep."

"I did, thank you."

"Excellent. We have a long day ahead of us." He pointed to the travel bag draped over her shoulder. "Let me take that for you."

"Thanks."

They made their way outside to a black Mercedes-AMG GT four-door coupe parked by the curb. Stanisław opened the door for her and Nostradamus, closed it once they were in, and placed the travel bag in the trunk. As he climbed into the front passenger seat, he shifted to look at her.

"This is Piotr, our driver."

A man in his mid-forties with a greying pompadour glanced into the rearview mirror. "Good morning, Miss Reynolds."

"Please, call me Tatyana."

"Who is your friend?"

Tatyana scratched the dog behind its ears. "This is Nostradamus."

"Good to meet you, boy."

Nostradamus wagged his tail.

"Is only one hundred kilometers to Treblinka. Sit back and enjoy ride."

Sixty miles, thought Tatyana. They should arrive in no time. Was she wrong?

The Polish countryside was beautiful, dotted with quaint villages connected by tree-lined roads. However, all the roads were only two lanes, the speed limit barely exceeded thirty kilometers, and every town had a roundabout in its center. They had already driven for more than two hours.

"How much further?" she asked.

"We're halfway there," said Stanisław.

"Why are there so many roundabouts?"

"Speed bumps," answered Piotr.

"I don't understand."

"After German invasion in 1941, Soviet Union no want to be invaded again, so they forced Poland to create small roads with many roundabouts to slow down NATO tanks. Poland was speed bump for anyone invading Russia."

"Is that true?"

Stanisław became embarrassed. "I'm afraid so."

"Well, it gives me a chance to see how beautiful your country is."

They drove for another two hours before Stanisław pointed to the sign that read The Nazi German Extermination and Labor Camp in English and Polish. "We're here."

Once in the parking lot, Piotr pulled the Mercedes into a spot by the refreshment stand and shut it down. Stanisław opened the door for Tatyana and Nostradamus, then retrieved her travel bag from the trunk.

"We'll be a little while," he said to Piotr.

"No problem." The driver got out, leaned against the hood, and lit a cigarette.

Tatyana placed a harness on Nostradamus and attached the leash. "I'm ready."

Stanisław motioned toward a large white building on the opposite side of the parking lot. "Let's head over to the museum. Our guide will meet us there."

"Guide?"

"The government arranged to have someone associated with the museum show us around and answer any questions."

When they entered the museum, Stanisław went over to the desk to tell the guide they had arrived while Tatyana and Nostradamus wandered through the viewing area. A plastic-enclosed diorama of the camp dominated the room. She walked around it slowly, studying the details. The arrival platform with a station was constructed like any other normal European one, the intention to deceive those about to be murdered. The wooden huts for processing the victims sat on either side of the main square. The ten-room gas chamber where the Nazis exterminated their victims with less dignity than one would show toward euthanizing an animal. The pits where the remains were buried. Opposite this assembly line of death, behind a fence topped with barbed wire and concealed by pine trees, sat the SS compound where these monsters lived like normal humans when not carrying out the Final Solution.

Stanisław stepped up beside her. "It's fascinating."

"What is?" asked Tatyana, slightly taken aback.

"That a camp as small as Treblinka could butcher so many people in a little over a year." Stanisław shook his head in disgust. "It makes you wonder how many more would have been killed if the war had lasted another year."

Tatyana moved on, unable to look at the display any longer. "There aren't many artifacts on display."

"That's because the Nazis destroyed everything associated with this place when they closed it down. The only things archaeological teams have been able to dig up are remains from the dead."

Tatyana stepped over to a military grey Olympia Robust typewriter in a wooden transit box atop a pedestal. "What's the significance of this?"

"The SS developed their own typewriters for drafting documents. Everything about this is the same as a normal typewriter except for one detail."

Stanisław pointed to the top row of keys. Just to the right of the nine key sat the one bearing the plus and minus symbols. The plus symbol had been replaced with SS runes.

Nostradamus whined and backed up.

"What's wrong, boy?"

He pulled on the leash, wanting to get away. Tatyana led him back toward the diorama.

"Hello," said an attractive middle-aged woman who approached. "I'm Beata. You must be Mr. Półtorzycki and Miss Reynolds."

"We are. Please, call me Stanisław."

"And you can call me Tatyana."

Beata crouched. "And who is this handsome boy?"

"That's Nostradamus."

"Oh. Can you predict the future?"

Nostradamus wagged his tail and barked once.

"If you're ready, then follow me."

The walk along the trail to the camp was pleasant, which seemed unusual given the location's history. Nostradamus stopped twice to relieve himself. When they broke into the clearing, Beata pointed to the series of cement blocks.

"That's where the rail line used to sit."

"Why does it extend beyond the camp into the woods?"

"The trains the Germans brought in were sixty cars in length. They would unload the first set of boxcars, and then the train would pull forward to unload the rest."

They followed the stone path up to the elevated area.

"This is the platform where the people were unloaded." Beata pointed to the area to the left of the stones. "That's where the phony train station stood. It was designed to give those arriving a false sense of security, to make them think they were being relocated and not be put to death. Follow me."

They made their way along the stone path leading from the platform. Off to the right sat six marble stones with polished surfaces. Each stone had a different word chiseled in it: Polska, Czechoslowacja, Francja, Jugoslawia, ZSRR, and Belgia. Off to the left sat five stones bearing the names Austria, Bułgaria, Niemcy, Grecja, and Macedonia.

"What are those?"

"They represent the different ethnic groups killed here. The camp was intended primarily to complete the Final Solution, but others were included in the gassings."

"Disgusting."

"I agree. It was a dark time across the continent." Beata led the way along the stone path.

They came upon an open area thirty acres in size surrounded by trees. A tall monolith composed of scores of huge granite blocks erected to resemble the Wailing Wall in Jerusalem sat in the center of the clearing, constructed in such a way that a large crack ran down its center. In front of the memorial, a polished granite block sat at an angle with the words NEVER AGAIN chiseled on its surface in English, German, French, Polish, Russian, Hebrew, and Yiddish. Four areas that looked like cemeteries extended from the monolith, each with marble stones of various sizes and polished surfaces similar to the ones they had just passed. Each had a name etched onto it. Tatyana walked over to the nearest stone, which bore the word Warsaw.

Beata stepped up beside her. "There are seventeen thousand such stones on the memorial site. Most represent the maximum number of people who could be killed on any given day. Two hundred and sixteen of them bear the name of a city or town in Poland where Jews were rounded up and sent here. The different sizes of those stones correlate to the number of

Jews seized in each area."

Tatyana looked around, incredulous. "Almost half the field is covered in stones."

"Poland suffered terribly under the Nazis."

"Excuse me," interrupted Stanisław. "Why are there four separate areas? Why not arrange them in rows like in a cemetery?"

"Because these stones were placed on the sites of the pits where the gassed bodies of the deceased were buried. There were eleven of them when the camp was torn down. The stones were arranged to show where and how large the pits were. The ashes of nearly a million people are buried beneath those stones."

"Dear God," muttered Stanisław.

"It gives you an idea of how far the Nazis carried out their brutality. No one realizes the scope of the atrocities committed until they see it firsthand."

Tatyana closed her eyes and focused her attention on the area's spiritual essence. She braced herself, expecting the souls of the nearly one million slaughtered here to reach out to her, begging for help. Surprisingly, that did not happen. She did sense a spectral presence, one larger than any she had experienced before, but it lingered in the background, remaining dormant and subdued. Almost submissive, as if the trapped spirits were afraid to reveal themselves.

For a brief moment, Tatyana also perceived a malevolent darkness unlike anything she had dealt with previously. Upon being detected, the darkness receded into the background, becoming nothing more significant than a slight hum. She wrote it off as being part of the disturbing aura associated with this place.

Nostradamus also sensed the darkness. The dog whimpered and moved against Tatyana's leg, his eyes looking up at Tatyana as if pleading to leave immediately.

"Have you ever received reports of people being contacted

by the spirits residing here?"

"All the time. Our curator, Krystyna, is extremely acceptable to the spirit world. She visited the camp once and was so
disturbed by it she never returned. She spends her time
working in the museum. If you want my opinion, those three
assholes who came here a few weeks ago to turn this site into a
propaganda campaign were murdered by the spirits. And it
served them right."

"Have the spectral levels been increased since the incident?"

"I can't tell for sure. I have no connection with the other
side. A ghost could be standing behind me, slapping me on the
back of my head, and I wouldn't know."

"There are none connected to you," said Tatyana.

"That's good to know. Since the incident, Krystyna has felt
a greater disturbance than usual around here. When she found
out you were coming today, she took the day off, afraid of what
might happen." Beata's expression did not change. "Let me
show you something."

They walked diagonally across the field until they reached a
rectangular area covered with crushed black basalt cemented
together, symbolizing burnt charcoal.

"What's this?" asked Stanisław.

"One of the cremation pits where the bodies were burned.
The Nazis did not want to waste the time and resources to
build a crematorium like at Auschwitz, so they did it the
primitive way."

Stanisław closed his eyes and turned away.

"You've never been here before?" asked Beata.

He shook his head.

"Well, you should have." Beata turned and motioned toward the monolith. "That marks the site of the gas chambers."

Tatyana felt an unsettling in her psyche. Voices called out
to her in many languages. She could not understand the words
but knew they wanted her to come closer.

"You two wait here while I check it out." Tatyana gently tugged on the leash. "Come on, boy."

Nostradamus refused to move. She tugged again, this time slightly harder. The dog stepped back until the leash was taut, then laid down on his stomach.

"What's wrong?"

Nostradamus fixed his stare on the monolith and growled.

Tatyana crouched beside her dog and scratched behind his ears. "You stay here, boy. I'll be back in a minute."

Nostradamus fixed his gaze on her and whimpered.

Tatyana stood and handed Nostradamus' leash to Stanisław. "Do you mind?"

"Of course not." Stanisław took the leash and gently rubbed the dog's side.

Beata placed a gentle hand on Tatyana's arm. "Be careful."

"Thanks." Tatyana patted the woman's hand, swallowed hard, and slowly made her way to the monolith.

Nick appeared by the structure, staring up at it. As she drew closer, he said, "You don't want to do this."

"I have to."

"The vibe here is worse than anything we've encountered before. It's extremely angry and hateful. Even I'm bothered by it."

"I must know."

Nick frowned and stepped back several feet. "God knows I can't stop you. But I'm here for you."

"I appreciate that."

Tatyana paused three feet from the monolith. Nick was right. Unlike the subdued hum from earlier, the site now emanated an anger and hatred she had never sensed before, but not toward her. It was directed at the victims' tormentors. The suffering and indignity they had endured. The way their tragedy was practically forgotten by history. Clos a million souls cried out to her, begging her to touch the monolith, to experience their tragedy. Common sense warned Tatyana not to do this, that she was unprepared to handle a spectral experience of this magnitude.

Her humanity told her otherwise. She needed to understand their suffering if she hoped to free their souls.

Tatyana inched closer and lifted her right hand. The spectral energy emanating from the monolith tingled against her fingers. Breathing deeply, she stepped forward and placed her palm on the marble surface.

A terror Tatyana had never conceived possible overwhelmed her soul. Her lungs closed down. She struggled to remain calm and resume breathing. As she did, a flood of mental imagery inundated her mind, images from the camp's dark past, the horror closing down Tatyana's senses.

CHAPTER SIX

C YNA HAD NOT slept for two days since her family had been shoved into one of sixty railroad box cars at Warsaw's train station to be transferred to a transit camp where they would be processed and relocated to the countryside. She wanted to sleep, but so many people were crowded in the box car, at least one hundred by her estimate, she could barely breathe, let alone lie down. Maybe she wasn't innovative enough. A young boy beside them had napped for the last three hours by wedging himself between his parents.

Even if she could sleep standing up, Cyna doubted she could because of the stench. Being confined to the Warsaw Ghetto for more than a year slowly wore away at everyone's cleanliness. Being stuffed into the boxcar like cattle only accelerated that process. The summer heat made everyone in the confined area sweat which, after two days, created the foulest body odor she had ever smelled. Even that was preferable to the stench of urine and feces. The only toilet the Nazis had provided was a bucket in the far corner, and since it was too cramped to move about, many people relieved themselves where they stood. When the old woman beside her shat herself, Cyna almost puked.

Cyna became anxious as the train slowed. Anxiety turned to joy when a teenage boy by the only window in the box car stood on his toes and called out to the others, "We're here."

The train slowed and came to a stop with a slight jolt. A commotion broke out on the platform. A few seconds later, the side door slid open, allowing in sunlight and, even better, fresh air. It felt so good to breathe again.

A German soldier in a grey uniform stood to the left, calling, "*Raus! Raus!*" Everyone grabbed their suitcases and filed out of the boxcar, forming a large group on the platform.

Cyna looked around. The place seemed nice, much prettier than the ghetto in Warsaw. Pine trees surrounded the area, and birds chirped in the branches. It had been a long time since she had seen either. The German soldiers on the platform were dressed in the same grey uniforms as those in the city but acted nicer. Even the station itself seemed friendly. Soothing music piped through speakers. The brick building ran the length of the platform, with potted flowers hanging every few feet apart. Signs showed the directions to Bialystok, Baranowicze, and Wojkowice, although she had no idea where those places were. An antique, ornate clock was mounted on the wall above the entrance. Beneath it hung a sign announcing their destination: TREBLINKA.

Her father was pleased they had arrived safely. Her mother, on the other hand, had that same look of concern mixed with fear she had shown since being relocated to the ghetto.

"This looks like a nice place."

"I hope so, dear." Her mother wrapped an arm around Cyna and hugged her.

A boy no more than six years old stood nearby in a sailor's uniform. Behind her, a man in a suit straightened his necktie to look presentable. Off to the right, a young mother adjusted the blanket around her baby to keep it warm, whispering it would soon be over.

Cyna turned around and looked back into the boxcar. Seven people had laid down and fallen asleep. She hoped they would wake up in time to join the others.

Glancing forward, Cyna saw the engineer leaning out the window, watching everyone disembark. He was an older man with greying hair, a wrinkled face, and a sullen expression. He glanced in her direction. Cyna smiled and waved. The grumpy old man did not wave back, instead taking his index finger and running it across his throat.

A tall man in a grey uniform, with blonde hair, blue eyes, and a pleasant smile, stepped in front of the crowd and spoke to them in Polish.

"Welcome to Treblinka. You'll be processed here before being assigned to your final destination. Because there's an infestation of lice in Warsaw, we're going to shave your heads so it doesn't spread to the farms. After that, you'll all receive a shower and be issued your new assignments. Follow me, please."

The arrives passed through a gate and entered a broad square surrounded on three sides by fences that were three meters high and topped with barbed wire. When everyone was inside, the pleasant man stopped.

"Leave your belongings here. Take only your identification and valuables."

A rabbi asked, "What will happen to them? What if they're misplaced or stolen?"

"Remember where you place them. You can come back and retrieve them once the processing is over. *Raus! Raus!*"

Cyna's mother paused long enough to remove the family's identification papers and a small purse with jewelry from their suitcase.

"What about my doll?"

"It'll be safe here." For some reason, her mother did not sound convincing.

"I don't want her to get lost. Please."

Her mother forced a smile, removed the doll from the suitcase, and handed it to Cyna. The girl held it tightly.

The group entered a second square with one hut on the left and three on the right. More men in uniforms, some of them holding the leashes of German Shepherds, mingled around the edges. Cyna and her family waited in line for several minutes before it was their turn to step up to a desk. A surly soldier sat behind it.

"ID and valuables."

"Will they be safe?" asked Cyna's mother.

The man flashed her a dirty look. "We're not thieves like you."

He jotted down a few notes and handed her mother a piece of paper. "Here's the voucher for your things. Don't lose it."

Her mother took the slip and slid it into her pocket.

After a few minutes, the pleasant soldier called out again.

"Break into two groups. The men will stay here. The women and children will head to the barracks on the left."

"Why can't I stay with my husband?" a woman off to the right shouted.

"It'd be improper to have men and women showering together. Please, do as you're told."

Tears flowed down her mother's face. She hugged her father, refusing to let go.

"I love you."

Her father broke the grip. "We'll be together soon. Don't make such a fuss."

Inside the barracks, another soldier stood near the door. This one had a stern expression on his face. "*Achtung!* Everyone must leave their shoes here. Tie the laces together so they don't get separated. Take off your socks and stockings and place them in your shoes. Then strip down and leave your clothes on the hooks above your shoes. Take off everything, including your underwear. After that, see the hairdressers. *Raus!*"

Cyna and her mother obliged along with the other women. Cyna would miss her socks. Her grandmother had knitted them as a gift for her several years ago. Oh, well. She grabbed her doll and followed her mother.

They headed over to where the other women were undressing, the younger ones embarrassed over being naked around the soldiers. The men in grey uniforms did not care, more interested in moving the process along rather than gawking at the nude bodies.

Rows of female hairdressers were inside the barracks. Each naked woman went up to one and had their hair removed with clippers. One middle-aged lady asked, "Why are you doing this?"

"To prevent the spread of lice," was the curt reply. When finished, she directed the woman to the other side of the barracks.

A young woman nearby ran her hand across her head after the cropping. "This feels uneven. Could you trim it out a bit, please?"

The hairdresser quickly obliged and moved her along.

Behind Cyna, a young woman whispered to her friend, "I told you. Why would they cut our hair if they wanted to kill us?"

"Maybe you're right," her friend admitted reluctantly.

"Of course, I'm right. Relax. You'll feel better after the shower."

Cyna heard them but ignored the conversation.

Soon, they were next in line, with an elderly woman in front of them.

"I don't have hair. I wear a wig."

"Take it off," ordered the hairdresser, her hand extended. The elderly woman obliged. She was practically bald, with tufts of messed up, short hair across her scalp. The hairdresser waved her on and pointed to Cyna and her mother. "Next."

It bothered Cyna to see the man cutting off her mother's hair. She had such beautiful auburn locks. Cyna used to love cuddling with her mother and sniffing the shampoo whenever she washed it. She had not done that since moving into the ghetto.

It was Cyna's turn. She sat stoically while the woman chopped off her hair. When she was finished, she joined her mother and smiled. "Now we really do look alike."

Her mother smiled and took her hand.

Once everyone had been processed and given a towel and a bar of soap, the pleasant soldier who had led them into the barracks moved to the rear door.

"Listen up. Take your towel, soap, valuables, and papers with you and follow me."

The women and children were led out of the rear door of the barracks to a small booth. A *scharführer* leaned out the ticket window.

Suddenly, the men in grey uniforms became violent. They ripped away the towels and knocked the bars of soap out of the prisoners' hands. One by one, the adults were forced to the window where the *scharführer* took their bag of valuables and their identification papers, placing the former in bins and tearing up and tossing away the latter. The soldiers sped up the process by forcibly removing jewelry still being worn. One of the bad men grabbed a middle-aged woman's earrings and tore them off, ripping out pieces of her ear. Another tried to take the wedding ring off an older woman. When it did not slip off easily, the man broke the woman's finger and removed the ring.

Panic spread through the women and children. Even Cyna became frightened.

Once stripped of their remaining belongings, the woman and children were formed into five lines and ushered down a curved walkway flanked on each side by flowers and fir trees, with barbed wire on the other side, the ground covered in white sand. More men in uniforms lined the walkway. Two soldiers stood by the gate, laughing and conversing in German. Cyna had learned some German while in the ghetto, but the only words she made out were *Himmel Strasse*—the Road to Heaven. She had a sick feeling that, despite the name, they were not going to a nice place.

The men kept screaming at them. "*Schneller! Schneller!*"

Children had to run to keep up with their parents.

The path opened into a clearing with a cement building in

the center. A pillar of dark smoke and an acrid smell came from behind the building. Off to the right sat several mounds of sand and an excavator digging earth out of the ground. More soldiers stood by, practically pushing the people inside the building as they yelled, "*Schneller! Schneller!*"

Some of the soldiers held Alsatians on leashes. They moved forward, allowing the dogs to attack the crowd, biting their legs and tearing off chunks of flesh. The men without dogs closed in, hitting the slower women and children with the butts of their weapons to make them move faster. The mass of terrified people pushed Cyna and her mother into the building.

Inside were ten steel doors. The soldiers shoved the people ahead of her into the first door. Cyna counted those entering the chamber. Almost four hundred people were stuffed in. The soldiers closed the steel door, securing it with several bolts and locks.

Cyna and her mother were among those forced into the second chamber. It was not that big, only seven meters by seven meters, yet more people were constantly shoved in until those inside could not move, their bodies pushing against one another. Still, more people entered. Cyna was shoved against a woman in front of her. A woman with a small boy crushed her from behind.

"Stop that," cried Cyna. "It hurts."

The boy did not respond.

Off to the left, a sound like bones snapping echoed through the chamber, followed by a child screaming, "My chest hurts."

When the last person had entered, the soldiers closed the door and bolted it. Something that sounded like a car engine started, and Cyna prepared herself for the shower, hoping the water would not be cold.

No water came out of the shower heads.

"Are the showers broken, mom?"

"I don't think so, dear." The mournful waver in her mother's voice caused Cyna to panic.

Off to the right, a little girl about three years old began coughing and gasping for air. She went limp. The girl's mother screamed and tried to revive the child but soon began coughing herself. More children and shorter women began choking. The old woman who had given up her wig stopped breathing and collapsed against the people surrounding her.

Cyna coughed.

"It'll be okay, hon. Just close your eyes and relax."

Cyna felt strange. For some reason, she suddenly developed a throbbing headache and became disoriented.

"Mommy, I don't feel good. Hold me."

"I can't, dear," sobbed her mother, unable to move because of all the other people crammed around her, instead trying to reach out to hold her daughter's hand.

"Please, help me. I'm scared—"

Cyna went into convulsions. Thankfully, she quickly became unconscious, sparing her from further suffering. A few moments later, she suffocated.

It took another five minutes for the remaining women and children to join her.

DANIEL STEPPED OFF the boxcar onto the platform, part of the second group to disembark. Like the others, they were yelled at and pushed around by the SS troopers, herded into the main square, and forced to leave their luggage behind. Daniel stood behind an older man who was hunched over and barely walking with a cane. The older man called out to one of the guards.

An SS officer came over. Two soldiers followed, carrying a stretcher.

"Go with these men. They'll take good care of you."

"Thank you."

The two men helped the older man onto the stretcher, lifted him, and made their way to the square's southeast corner to an area separated by trees. Behind them stood a building with a white flag bearing a Red Cross. Daniel had found a way to avoid hard labor for a while if he could only convince the SS officer to let him go to the infirmary.

Pretending to cough, he stepped over to the officer. "Excuse me, I'm recovering from pneumonia. It'll be a few days before I'm back on my feet. May I be allowed to go to the infirmary?"

The German broke into a huge grin. "Of course. Follow me."

He led Daniel to the structure. Daniel fought back the urge to smile. He might get to sleep in a soft bed tonight and maybe even have a decent meal.

They passed through a walled enclosure and turned left into the infirmary. It did not appear like a hospital at all. There were no beds, no medical equipment, no doctors or nurses. Even more strange, the SS officer continued across the room and exited through a door on the right. Daniel followed, walked several feet, and stopped.

A pit had been dug into the ground. Several corpses lay strewn around it, bullet holes in their heads. The two guards carrying the older man on the stretcher stopped by the pit's edge. An SS officer stepped over, placed his Lugar against the older man's head, and pulled the trigger. The body shook from the concussion. As the officer stepped aside, the two men flipped up the left edge of the stretcher, tossing the body into the pit. It rolled down the side, coming to an obscene rest among the other corpses.

"What the hell is—"

Daniel spun around in time to see the SS officer holding a Lugar aimed at his skull. He watched in shock as the officer pulled the trigger. Daniel's lifeless body tumbled down the incline to join the older man.

THE LAST TWENTY boxcars to be unloaded contained a bunch of surly people who had been stuck in there the longest as they waited for the others to be processed. It felt like forever before the train moved forward for a third time. It lurched to a stop, and the doors finally opened.

An SS officer stood on the platform, waving his arm for them to exit. "*Raus! Schnell!*"

Ezra stumbled onto the platform, nearly tripping after being stuck inside for so long.

"Watch it, Jew," snapped the officer.

Ezra lowered his head and blended in with the other prisoners.

A middle-aged woman whom Ezra recognized as being in his apartment building in Warsaw staggered out of the boxcar.

The SS officer ran up to her. "*Schneller!*"

"I'm going as fast as I can," she stammered.

"It's not fast enough." The officer shoved the woman, knocking her over.

A tall man wearing a *kippah* went to help her, but the officer shoved him aside.

"She can get up on her own."

"Show some kindness."

"Move!"

"Is that any way to treat workers?" The tall man looked toward the station, and his eyes widened. "What's that pillar of black smoke?"

"None of your business." The SS officer shoved him along. "*Schnell!*"

The tall man stood defiant. "I used to work at a funeral home. It smells like burnt flesh. What are you burning?"

A wave of fear flowed through the prisoners.

"I'll shut you up."

The SS officer reached for his pistol but was stopped when a loud and commanding voice came from near the station. A tall, handsome SS officer with a Saint Bernard beside him made his way to the outburst. He grinned sardonically.

The first SS officer snapped to attention and stood back. "Sorry, *Untersturmführer* Franz."

Franz waved him off. "I have this."

The handsome SS officer walked around the tall man, looking him up and down, enjoying the way the Jew trembled with fear. Ezra noticed the wet spot on the front of the man's pants. The officer completed the circle, stared down the tall man, then stepped back a few feet.

"Barry, *Mensch fasten Hund.*"

The Saint Bernard lunged, knocked over the tall man, and sunk its jaws into his groin. The man screamed in agony as the dog ravaged his private parts. Blood mixed with the urine on the front of his pants. After a few seconds of torment, the SS officer issued another command.

"Barry, *kommst hier.*"

The Saint Bernard stopped its attack and rejoined its master, sitting peacefully by his side as if nothing had happened. Franz looked over to the younger SS officer. "Proceed."

"Move it unless you want to join the other Jew!"

Terrified that they might be next, the prisoners on the platform grabbed their belongings and headed for the main square.

Only then did Ezra realize that they were not being relocated but were going to be butchered. Resigned to his fate, his spirits finally broken by years of Nazi persecution, he picked up his suitcase and followed the others to their death.

GIDEON RUMMAGED THROUGH the abandoned clothes, most still warm after being stripped off those sent to the gas chamber, sorting out those still fit to wear. Little would be discarded since the Germans considered all their plunder valuable. Other Jews would remove the yellow Stars of David and then pack them, along with the shoes and socks, to be transported back to Germany for those civilians who had lost everything in the

Allied bombings.

Gideon was one of the two-hundred-person "red team," so-called because of the red armbands they wore, which were created to sort through the victims' belongings. The team was comprised of those Jews in fit condition who had been pulled aside from each arrival and worked until they were no longer of use. They then joined those murdered, though their demise would be a merciful bullet to the head. His brother Jakob used to work alongside him until the horror of what he did to his fellow man overwhelmed him. One morning, they found Jakob hanging from the barracks beam on a noose made of discarded clothes tied together. Gideon knew he would be joining him soon enough.

Gideon's team, along with a few other groups, were the machinery behind the Nazi exploitation of mass extermination. Nothing confiscated from those who entered the front gate went to waste. Everything taken from the victims—clothes, money, gold and jewelry, eyeglasses, furniture, toys—had value in Germany. His friend Ira, one of the hairdressers, told him the shaved hair was returned to be used as filling for mattresses and to make saddles.

ZALMAN WATCHED AS the *untersturmführer* peered through the tiny peephole into the gas chamber, making sure everyone inside was dead. He stepped back and motioned to Zalman.

"Open it."

Zalman rushed forward, undid the bolts and locks, and pulled aside the metal door. Half a dozen bodies tumbled out onto the platform. Their faces all had a pale-yellow hue to them. An old lady, probably someone's grandmother, landed at his feet. Blood dripped from her nose and mouth. Urine and feces dripped down her legs.

Two Jews raced over, picked up the body of a young woman, and carried her to the trolley that sat a few feet away, stopping only long enough to have one of the dentists check for gold teeth. Zalman's brother Chaim was one of the dentists. He forced open the woman's mouth and, when he found a gold filling, tore it out with a pair of pliers. Chaim had been assigned to this nightmarish task when they first arrived two weeks ago. Once, he had missed finding a gold tooth in a corpse and was whipped forty times before being sent back to work.

Zalman and his comrade lifted the body of a naked ten-year-old girl from the pile of asphyxiated corpses and carried her outside. As they passed by the *untersturmführer*, the girl moaned.

"Put her down," demanded the SS officer.

They obeyed. The *untersturmführer* unholstered his Lugar and fired a single round into her head. Zalman and his comrade picked up the body, placed it on the trolley, and went back to the gas chamber.

This time, they picked up the body of a teenager. As they left, Zalman's comrade stepped in a mound of feces, dropping its legs onto the concrete. The *untersturmführer* rushed over and repeatedly whipped Zalman's comrade on the shoulders with his baton.

"Hurry up, Jew. You're slowing things down."

Zalman cringed, waiting for the *untersturmführer* to beat him. Instead, after lashing his comrade twenty-five times, the German kicked him in the ass as they carried away the body. Two more Jews raced in to remove the next body.

"I'd love to throw that bastard into the pit."

"Shut up." Zalman glanced up at his comrade. "If they hear you, we'll both be killed."

"It would be preferable than doing this."

Zalman agreed. Several times, Zalman had considered tossing himself into the pit and ending this nightmare. Only his religious beliefs kept him from committing suicide.

When the trolley was full, Zalman and his comrade pushed

it along the narrow-gauge tracks to the pit where the corpses were cremated. Every time Zalman approached it, his stomach churned, even though he had been doing this for over a week. Despite the rag he wore across his face, the stench of the acrid smoke seeped through, sickening him. But not as much as his participation in this disgusting act of inhumanity.

The pit was one of six constructed at the camp. It had been dug several hundred meters in length and two meters in width, with the bottom lined with six iron rails thirty meters long. The victims of the morning train still lined the bottom. Once twenty-five hundred bodies filled the void, the mass would be covered with wood, doused with kerosene, and set on fire.

When the trolley was unloaded, Zalman and his comrade returned to the gas chamber, passing by another pit that still crackled in the flames. Zalman avoided looking in, not wanting to watch the bodies shrivel and contract under the flame's heat. That did not stop him from hearing the sizzling as the body fat burned in the inferno. They would feed the fire with human detritus all afternoon, then wait four hours for the bodies to burn completely. Once the pit had cooled off enough to work, excavators would empty it and transfer the ashes to another pit for disposal.

Zalman and his comrade pushed the trolley back to the gas chamber, where more bodies were removed and loaded for disposal.

This process would continue tomorrow, the day after, and the day after that until Zalman was of no further use. Then, he would be executed and thrown in with the others.

"JEW!" YELLED THE *unterscharführer*. "You missed one. Are you trying to sabotage us?"

Teodor shuddered, expecting a beating. When none oc-curred, a miracle in itself, he jumped over the side of the pit with his bucket and raced down the yellow sand to retrieve the skull uncovered by the excavator. Plunging his way through the ankle-deep dirt, he reached the bottom, barely avoiding being hit by the excavator's shovel that never paused. A cloud of large, obnoxious flies hovered around the skull. Teodor brushed them away and tossed the skull into his bucket. Several teeth had been knocked loose from the jaw and lay in the dirt. He glanced up. Neither the *unterscharführer* nor the officer he chatted with were paying attention, so Teodor left the teeth there so future generations would know of the nightmare that took place within these forty acres of land. Heading up the side of the pit, he barely got out of the way before the excavator turned up more dirt.

As part of the *Knochen-Kolonne,* or the Bone Brigade, Teodor's role was to remove any bones or body parts discovered during the dig and bring them to the fire pit. When first established, Treblinka did not have a crematorium and instead buried its victims in pits. However, the German defeat at Stalingrad and the advance of the Red Army compelled the camp to destroy all evidence of its existence. The problem was, in addition to the two trainloads of victims that arrived daily, they now had to unearth eleven pits previously dug on the compound, which contained the corpses of those murdered. Teodor had the honor of working at the fourth-largest pit, which housed a quarter of a million bodies.

As he reached the wall of the pit, something gave way under his feet. The decomposed body of a child popped up through the sand, striking Teodor in the legs. Teodor cried out, surprised by its sudden appearance.

The *unterscharführer* heard and glanced into the pit, his hand around the whip, ready to punish Teodor for any mistake he made. Instead, on seeing the decayed body, he snapped his fingers and pointed to a pair of Jews along the rim.

"Pay attention and get that thing out of here."

The two grabbed a ladder-like stretcher, raced down the pit wall, and hoisted the body onto it amidst a burst of fly activity.

Lifting it, they struggled to climb up without dropping the decayed carcass, which, at minimum, would have incurred a beating. Once over the rim, they hurried away with the stretcher to dispose of its contents in the fire pit.

Teodor continued walking through the pit, searching for any bone fragments that needed to be removed.

Deep down, he prayed that someday the world would know what happened at Treblinka.

CHAPTER SEVEN

TATYANA WOKE UP with a start, bolting upright. The images she had perceived still haunted her thoughts, and the anger and fear from hundreds of thousands of souls still remained with her. For some reason, she had become used to it.

Only then did Tatyana realize she was lying on a sofa inside the museum. Nick leaned against the opposite wall, a look of concern on his face. Nostradamus sat on the floor beside her. On seeing his mistress awake, he stood, placed his front paws on the sofa, and licked her face.

Tatyana scratched him behind the ears. "I'm okay, boy."

"Are you sure?" asked Stanisław, who sat in a chair beside her.

Tatyana nodded. "How long have I been out?"

"Almost an hour," answered Beata, who stood nearby.

Swinging her legs off the sofa, Tatyana tried to stand. Dizziness overwhelmed her, so she sat down again. "What happened?"

"You touched the monolith, gasped for air for several seconds, then fainted. Beata called a couple of groundskeepers, who brought you back here to Krystyna's office. We were worried."

"Thanks, but I'll be fine. I just need a minute to rest." The traumatic emotions had subsided a bit. However, the vile images she had witnessed would stay with her forever.

"What did you see?" asked Nick.

"Hundreds of thousands of spirits are trapped here, more

than I've ever dealt with. They all relayed their experiences at the camp."

"All at once?" asked Beata.

Tatyana nodded.

"Dear God. No wonder you passed out."

"Will you be able to help them?" asked Stanisław.

"Yes. Only I don't know how yet. Help me up, please."

Stanisław rose from the chair, took Tatyana by the arm, and assisted her in standing. She wobbled for a second but quickly regained her footing.

"I'm okay now. Thanks."

They exited the office into the main portion of the museum.

"I've read numerous accounts of what happened here from the few who survived," said Beata. "I can't imagine experiencing such nightmares."

"It was horrifying." Tatyana stopped in front of the diorama and stared at it, the images from each location playing out in her mind. "The worst part was experiencing the emotions those people went through. The fear. The desperation. The agony."

"There's something you're not telling us," said Nick from the other side of the display.

Damn, he knew her too well. Tatyana turned to face Stanisław and Beata. "Amongst the anguish of the victims, I detected another feeling. Something malevolent."

"The spirits of the teenagers?" asked Stanisław.

"No. This was strong, confident, intelligent. The fact that it could make its way to me through the other sensations meant it must also be extremely powerful."

From across the museum came a clacking that sounded like the keys of a typewriter. They all stared at the typewriter in the display case. The keys moved on their own, slowly, one at a time. When the typing stopped, the carriage return moved by itself, raising the platen up three spaces and centering the paper. Tatyana walked over. Three words had been typed.

you are correct

Stanisław turned to Beata. "Please tell me that the type-writer working on its own is part of the display."

She shook her head. "I wish it was."

Tatyana motioned for them to be quiet. She sensed the same dark presence that had hung around the camp, increasing in intensity inside the museum. "Are you the malevolent spirit I detected at the monument?"

More typing and the carriage return moved.

malevolent is offensive

"Fine. Are you the strong spirit I detected?"

Three keys moved, and the x rolled up.

yes

"Did you want to talk with me?"

Two keys moved, and the carriage return moved the page up three spaces.

no

"Then what do you want from me?"

The procedure repeated itself.

to leave

Tatyana glanced over at Nick and whispered. "Do you know who this is?"

Nick shrugged. "All I know for certain is that it's the same spirit from the camp."

Tatyana glanced over at Beata. "Has this happened before?"

"No one has ever reported anything like this."

Tatyana turned back to the typewriter. "Why do you want

me to leave? I'm here to help."
More typing.

> **your help is not necessary**

"Don't you want to be freed from this place?'
More typing.

> **we do not want to leave**

"Are there more than one of you?"
More typing.

> **yes**

"How many?"

> **several**

Tatyana was confused. "Who are you?"

A long pause ensued. At first, Tatyana thought the spirit had left, but she sensed its presence in the room. Then the keys typed twice. The transom moved up three spaces, leaving an answer that stunned everyone.

> **we are SS**

CHAPTER EIGHT

B EATA ESCORTED THE group out of the museum and onto the front lawn, where they gathered beneath a pine tree.

"What happened in there?" asked Stanisław, who was confused.

"The spirits of SS guards must still be here," explained Tatyana.

"I assume those were the malevolent spirits you encountered in the camp," asked Stanisław.

She nodded.

"Did they show you their experiences like the other spirits did?"

"No. I can only see what the spirits want me to. The SS remained quiet, which is why I only detected their essence. It was the victims who told their story."

"What about when they talked to you on the typewriter?" asked Beata.

"They kept their emotions concealed. I didn't realize they were SS until they told me."

Stanisław thought for a moment. "Are you sure they're SS and not someone pretending to be?"

"I have to take them at their word, but I can't imagine who else would reach out to me like that. No question they want me to leave, which means I pose a threat. And they possessed that same pompous brutality associated with the SS. Who else could it be?"

Stanisław shrugged. "Could it be the *kapos*? I've read that the Jewish guards who watched over the other inmates could be as cruel as the Germans."

"Except there were no *kapos* here," corrected Beata. "The only Jews kept alive were on work details assigned to various duties around the camp. They didn't need *kapos* to keep them in line. Those people were worked to death, literally."

Nick walked up behind Tatyana. "You're overlooking one important point. According to your research, no German guards ever died at Treblinka."

"Good point," she said.

"What's a good point?" asked Stanisław.

"Sorry. Just thinking out loud." She turned to Beata. "It was my understanding that none of the SS guards ever died at Treblinka."

"Officially, no German deaths had been recorded. However, in August 1943, an uprising took place involving seven hundred prisoners. The pits had been emptied of corpses, and the Germans were preparing to close the camp. The work details knew they were about to be executed, so they launched a massive escape. It was brutal. Less than two hundred escaped, and most of those were either hunted down by the Nazis or died of starvation in the woods. There are no records of German deaths, only a few casualties. However, rumors have existed that some SS officers died and their deaths covered up."

Tatyana contemplated the possibility. She would have to ask the SS spirits the next time she contacted them.

"Will you be able to cleanse Treblinka of these ghosts?" asked Beata hesitantly.

"I should be able to," said Tatyana. Then, another thought crossed her mind. "Has anyone before me tried to release the spirits trapped here?"

Beata shook her head. "Such a *bourgeoise* concept would never have been tolerated under the communist regime. And other than the incident a few weeks ago, we have had no serious problems."

"Why do you think they're still here?" asked Stanisław. "You'd think they'd want to leave."

"There could be a number of reasons. Spirits that experienced sudden deaths are often trapped in this realm, confused about what happened to them and unable to move on. Those who suffered violent deaths are sometimes trapped, their experiences linking them to their location. If there are SS officers here, they may be preventing the others from leaving. I've had many cases where evil spirits still have control over the good souls even after death."

"Are you sure you're up to this?" asked Stanisław.

"I'll do everything I can, though I'll be honest. It won't be easy."

Beata smiled. "We'll give you all the assistance we can."

"The same with my government," added Stanisław. "Just tell me what you need."

Nick shook his head in frustration. "You're not prepared for this one. You're dealing with an evil more malevolent than anything you've encountered."

Tatyana ignored him. "Could you drive me back to the hotel? I'll need time to plan my next move and gather the necessary supplies."

"Not a problem."

"Thanks." Tatyana turned to Beata. "I'll be back in a few days. I'm staying at the Marriott Warsaw Hotel. Let me know if there are any more paranormal incidents."

"I will. And thank you so much."

Beata grabbed Tatyana's hands, squeezed them tightly, and returned to the museum.

"If you're ready, I'll take you back now."

"Thanks."

Tatyana followed Stanisław back to the car. Piotr opened the rear door. Nostradamus crawled in the back and settled on the seat for a nap. Tatyana sat beside him and gently petted his side, trying to comfort him. The dog seemed more relaxed now that they had left the camp.

As they pulled out of the parking lot, Stanisław turned in his seat. "Do you think you can cleanse the spirits from this place?"

"I hope so. I only need to figure out how."

CHAPTER NINE

THE RIDE BACK to Warsaw was not as pleasant as the drive out, Tatyana's thoughts being preoccupied with the task at hand. She mentally went over the various aspects of the case, trying to determine the best course of action, but was unable to come up with a plan. She would need a lot more time.

She did not realize where they were until Piotr pulled up in front of the hotel.

"We're here."

"Already? Sorry I wasn't much company."

"Don't worry about it. You have a lot on your mind." Stanisław reached into his shirt pocket, withdrew a business card, turned it over, and scribbled something on the back. "Here's my phone number. Let me know when you're ready to go back or if you need help with anything. And feel free to call me anytime, day or night."

"I appreciate all you've done for me."

"It's my pleasure. Besides, you're doing my government a huge favor. Talk to you soon."

Tatyana woke up Nostradamus, walked him around the block, then returned to her hotel room. Nick waited for her on the sofa, watching Polish TV. Nostradamus ran over, jumped on the cushions beside him, and curled up for another nap.

"Have I told you that you're in way over your head?"

"Several times." Tayana draped her jacket over the back of a chair and then dropped into the loveseat beside the sofa. "Now you can help by offering some advice."

"I wish I could help. You're the paranormal investigator.

I'm your charming and handsome sidekick."

"You forgot to add modest."

Nick grinned. "Modesty is for those who should be modest."

It was the first time she had seen him in a good mood since they arrived in Poland.

"It's good to see you back to your old self."

"I know you. You're not going to walk away from this situation until you free those spirits from the camp. That won't be easy, but I'm here to help."

"Thanks." Tatyana leaned back into the loveseat. She could use a nap herself. "What's your take on the situation? And please don't tell me I'm in over my head."

"You know that already. There are hundreds of thousands of souls trapped at the camp. When the SS talked to you at the museum, I only detected three entities."

"At least the odds are in our favor."

"Don't count on it. The souls of the prisoners are still tormented by what they went through and are terrified of the SS officers still there. It's the same scenario as at Bethlehem Asylum. Dr. Savage ruled the place so brutally that even after their death, the patients who were stuck there feared him too much to challenge him."

Tatyana rubbed her eyes. "This is totally different."

Nick raised an eyebrow. "How so?"

"I can't believe three entities can control several thousand."

"Why not? A small number of SS guards sent a hundred and fifty thousand people to their deaths every day. If the prisoners aboard any one of those trains fought back, thousands of people might have made it out alive."

"Then why didn't they fight back?"

"The Nazis were smart. They knew that if they loaded Jews onto trains and took them to extermination camps, most of them would have revolted. Instead, the SS spent years breaking their spirits. Taking away their rights, their homes, their businesses. Degrading them. Forcing them to wear Stars of David. Sending them to ghettoes where they lived little better than animals. The Germans destroyed them physically and emotionally, instilling fear in them. By the time these people were marched into the gas chambers, they had no will left to resist. That same collapse of the human spirit has been carried over into the after realm."

"How do you know this?" asked Tatyana.

"You would have, too, if the spirits didn't all rush to relay their experiences at once and overwhelm your senses. I probed their minds, and everyone I came across felt that way. It was an undercurrent that ran through them."

Tatyana thought for a moment. "I don't buy it. Maybe their psychological collapse prevented some of them from moving on, but not so many."

Nick was obviously frustrated. "Let me ask you this. When all the spirits were relating their experiences, did any of them discuss the revolt against the guards?"

The question caught Tatyana off guard. "No."

"That's my point. The spirits of those who had the courage to stand up to the Nazis were strong enough not to be trapped at Treblinka when they died. The others are so broken in spirit they don't have the courage to move on."

"So, for me to release these people from their hell—"

"You must give them the emotional strength to move on willingly."

"Shit." The word was an understatement. A cloud of despair that washed over her. "Do you have any suggestions?"

"Not off the top of my head. Hopefully, now you understand why I warned you about accepting this case." Nick did not say it maliciously but with sympathy for Tatyana's situation. He pushed himself off the sofa. "Let me think about it for a bit and see what I can come up with."

"Thanks."

"You're welcome. We'll figure out a way to get through this

one."

Nick disappeared with his usual annoying fanfare.

Nostradamus looked up, whined, and joined Tatyana on the loveseat. He curled up and lay beside her, resting his head on her leg, his eyes showing sympathy for his mistress's plight. Tatyana leaned over, kissed the dog on his forehead, then scratched behind his ears.

"Nick's right, I'm in over my head."

Nostradamus raised his head and gave her a face bath.

After a few minutes, Tatyana got up from the loveseat and went over to the phone.

"Room service, could you please send a bottle of Absolut to Suite 601? Thanks."

CHAPTER TEN

T ATYANA HAD INTENDED to use the vodka to calm her nerves and erase the disturbing mental images from that afternoon. It had the opposite effect. When she finally fell into a drunken stupor on the sofa, her mind continually replayed the horrifying images she had experienced, making her sleep a drunken nightmare. She woke up in the afternoon of the next day with a sour stomach, a dry mouth, the worst hangover of her life, and no idea how she would release these tormented souls from their spiritual hell.

Rolling over, she bumped into Nostradamus, who was spread out beside her.

"Good morning, boy."

The dog twisted his head to the side, wagged his tail furiously, and whined.

"You have to go out, don't you?"

Nostradamus barked once and raced to the door. Since Tatyana had fallen asleep in her clothes, she did not need to dress, though she looked like something the cat had dragged in. Nostradamus was agitated on the walk to the elevator, the ride down to the first floor, and as they crossed the lobby. Outside, he ran over to the nearest lamppost and lifted his leg, going for well over a minute. Tatyana had no clue how he held it for so long.

Nostradamus finished and came over to his mistress, happy once again. Since the fresh air helped clear her head, Tatyana took him for a walk around the block, stopping at a nearby bakery to purchase a cup of hot coffee for herself and a pastry for her companion.

When they returned to the hotel room, Nick waited for them on the sofa.

"Come here, boy."

Nostradamus ignored his friend, focusing on the bag containing his treat. He poked it with his nose and glanced up at his mistress. Tatyana pulled the pastry out and held it in front of her. Nostradamus licked his lips and sat, his tail wagging. When she lowered the pastry, Nostradamus grabbed it in his mouth and ran into the corner to enjoy it.

Nick chuckled. "I take second place to pastry?"

"He has his priorities." Tatyana sat beside Nick, shifting in the seat to face him. "You should see how he reacts when I give him a chunk of cheese."

"Nothing for you?"

Tatyana held up her paper cup. "I got myself a coffee."

"Anything to eat?"

She shook her head. "I'm not hungry."

"I figured as much." Nick motioned to the nearly empty bottle of vodka on the coffee table. "Tough night?"

"Over time I've gotten used to speaking with spirits with tortured souls, but yesterday overwhelmed me."

"Because of the visions of what those people went through?"

"That and the number of spirits reaching out. It didn't help that the SS also contacted me." Tatyana shivered. "I drank last night to clear my head and instead dreamt all night about the brutal way they were murdered."

"War is hell."

"This wasn't war. This was genocide."

"Where do we go from here?"

"I was thinking about it when I took Nostradamus for his walk. You know from your own experience that souls are often attached to a location where they died violently. All they need is someone to recognize their suffering and free them."

"It's not always that easy. Remember, Kathleen kept us trapped at Eden Hollow, and Dr. Savage did the same with the spirits of those he tormented at Bethlehem Asylum."

"You're referring to the souls of the SS officers trapped at Treblinka?"

Nick nodded.

"I refuse to believe three malignant spirits can keep hundreds of thousands of souls at bay. Now that we know what we're up against, it should be fairly easy to release the spirits."

Nick seemed skeptical. "It might not be as easy as you think."

"I disagree. If we cleanse the area with sage and try to create positive vibes, I should be able to free them from this realm."

"What about the SS?"

Tatyana grimaced. "Their spirits can rot there for eternity."

"I'm referring to their interfering with you."

"I can handle three evil entities."

Nick remained unconvinced. "You're the boss. What's next?"

"I'm going to call Stanisław and ask if we can return there tomorrow. I didn't bring enough sage, so I'll find a metaphysical store tonight." Tatyana paused. "I assume I'll see you tomorrow?"

"Of course."

"Good. I'm going to take a shower, grab something to eat, and then stock up on sage."

"I'll leave you alone tonight and meet you at the camp tomorrow. And please..." Nick pointed to the bottle of vodka. "Lay off that shit. It won't help you."

"I don't plan on drinking anymore tonight. It did more harm than good."

"Smart move. Get a good rest. You'll need it. See you tomorrow."

Nick faded away without his usual fanfare.

Nostradamus lay in the corner. He had devoured the pastry in three bites and licked the crumbs off the carpet and the wrapper.

While her dog was preoccupied, Tatyana took her shower.

CHAPTER ELEVEN

T HE SHOWER HELPED Tatyana feel better. She arranged for
Stanisław to pick her up in the morning, then ordered a
chicken Caesar salad for dinner. Of course, Nostradamus
mooched most of the chicken. After taking the dog for a walk,
she left him in the room, made her way to the lobby, and asked
the concierge to recommend a reputable metaphysical shop.
Unlike in the States, such shops were not as prevalent in
Poland. He eventually found one in the Mokotów District on
the city's outskirts. After confirming the store was open, the
concierge called a taxi to pick her up and wait while Tatyana
went shopping.

On reaching the metaphysical store, the taxi driver pulled
into an empty space across the street. He turned in his seat to
face Tatyana and pointed to the building, speaking in broken
English.

"There."

"Thank you."

Tatyana climbed out of the back, hesitated a moment, then
leaned over beside the open driver's window.

"You'll wait for me, right?"

"*Tak.*" The driver turned off the engine. "I wait."

Tatyana was surprised at how out of place the store appeared, at least from the outside. The façade was old, dating
back to the 1940s or 1950s, and dominated by a dirty, plate-
glass window and matching door off to the right that had seen
better days. The mounted sign on the fascia above the window
had not been updated in God knows how long, the faded paint

of the word *aptekarz* barely visible against the background. The only indication of the store's purpose was a drawing of a pentacle taped to the right corner of the window.

A tarnished brass bell attached to the door rang as she entered, although no one seemed to be around to hear it. Only twenty feet wide, the interior seemed as antique as the exterior. It had no overhead lighting, instead being illuminated by a series of stained-glass Tiffany table lamps placed every ten feet along the twin rows of old, wooden display cases used at one time to show off jewelry. The lower half of the walls were comprised of faded wood paneling, with the upper half made of plaster that had not been painted in years, the cracks partially covered by metaphysical posters in Polish. A service counter, as old as everything else inside, stood at the far end of the store and, to its right, a small sitting area with two antique wing-backed chairs, a claw and ball foot table, and a stained-glass Tiffany floor lamp.

What caught Tatyana's attention even more than the quaintness of the surroundings was the contents of the display cases. Hundreds of crystals used in all aspects of metaphysical activities lined the shelves, the light from the lamps reflecting off their surface. Two cases to the right contained sage, vervain, and dozens of other plants and herbs used in cleansings. Tatyana whistled. While all the stores she had frequented in the States sold trinkets like jewelry with crystals embedded in them or fancy holders for burning incense, this shop only contained basic supplies. It was like an armory for paranormal investigators.

She was going to need it.

An attractive middle-aged woman with wavy auburn hair stepped out of the back room and smiled at Tatyana.

"*Dzień dobry. Jestem Maja. Czy mogę ci pomóc?*"

Tatyana had forgotten about the language barrier. "I'm sorry. I'm American. Do you speak English?"

"A little. My name is Maja. How may I assist you?"

"I'm Tatyana. I'm looking for items to perform a spiritual cleansing."

Tatyana approached the counter and held out her hand. Maja shook it, then quickly pulled her hand away, her pleasantness rapidly changing to fear. She backed up until she was against the wall.

"Is something wrong?" asked Tatyana.

"Please accept my apology. You have an evil aura around you that frightened me."

"You can sense the spirit realm?"

Maja nodded. "I have never experienced such an aura before."

"That's strange. I don't feel it."

"It's powerful but benign. It shields itself from you. But it's clearly present."

Tatyana was taken aback, not only by the aura's existence but also its ability to shield itself, not only from here but also from Nick and Nostradamus.

"That's good to know. I'm sorry if I scared you."

"Not a problem." Maja garnered her courage and moved back to the counter. "How may I assist you?"

"I'm doing a spiritual cleansing to release tormented spirits from an evil place and am looking for bundles of sage to ward off the dark presence hanging over the area."

"We have much sage. How much do you need?"

Tatyana made a quick calculation. "Forty-five bundles."

Maja's eyes widened. "Why so many?"

"I'm trying to cleanse Treblinka."

"The death camp?"

"Yes."

Maja's smile returned. "So, you're the American spiritualist who has flown in to purge the camp of its evil."

"You've heard about that?"

"Yes." Maja leaned close and whispered. "Rumors about the spiritual world travel through the metaphysical community

67

as fast as a ghost can travel through walls. Follow me."

Maja led Tatyana to one of the display cases holding the sage. She reached down to the cabinet underneath it, pulled out a box filled with sage, and counted out fifty bundles, which she placed in a bag.

"The last five are free. You will need them to cleanse yourself when you finish."

"Good idea. Let me pick up five bloodstone crystals if you have any."

"Of course. This way."

Maja moved over to the counters on the opposite side of the store. Moving the lamp closer to see better, she picked out the five largest bloodstones in the case and added them to the bag. They returned to the counter, where Maja rang up the sale, and Tatyana paid.

"Thank you for all your help."

"It's my pleasure." Maja suddenly grew serious. "Please, be careful. You are dealing with an unimaginable evil, an evil that does not care at all for human life."

"I will. Thanks again."

Tatyana exited the shop and climbed back into the taxi. On the drive back to the hotel, she peered into her bag, confident she had everything necessary to cleanse Treblinka.

CHAPTER TWELVE

S TANISŁAW AND PIOTR picked up Tatyana and Nostradamus at six the following day to get an early start. No one
spoke much at the beginning of the drive. Tatyana struggled
not to fall asleep as Piotr negotiated through rush hour traffic.
Nostradamus sat on the seat beside his mistress, enjoying the
view. Once they had cleared the city and the road opened,
Stanisław initiated small talk.

"Sorry for the delay. Every year, the traffic in Warsaw gets
worse."

"This is nothing. You should see it in New York City or Los
Angeles."

"I guess it's one of the downsides of capitalism." Stanisław
laughed at his own joke, then glanced into the rearview mirror.
"I assume you've figured out a way to exorcise the ghosts at
Treblinka."

Tatyana did not correct him. "Yes. Every spirit that is stuck
at Treblinka met terrifying, violent deaths. Their spirits are still
scared and confused. Once I clear the camp of its bad essence,
I can encourage them to move on into the afterlife."

"It's that simple?"

"Surprisingly, yes. Sometimes all the spirits need is for
someone to recognize their suffering and give them permission
to depart."

"Then this will be a boring chapter in your memoirs."

"Memoirs?"

"Yes. You are writing memoirs about your cases, aren't
you?"

"Honestly, I hadn't thought about it until you mentioned the idea."

"You'd make a lot of money. I hear those books are best sellers in your country. Who knows, you might even get your own reality TV show someday."

God, I hope I never sell out like that, thought Tatyana.

"If you do get your own show, have me on an episode. My mother would be so proud to see her son on American television." Stanisław chuckled at the idea.

"It's a deal."

Nostradamus yawned, curled up on the seat beside his mistress, and took a nap. Tatyana agreed that it was a good idea.

"If you don't mind, I'm going to take a nap."

"No problem. I'll wake you when we arrive."

The lulling motion of the car quickly put her to sleep.

✕ ✕ ✕

"WE'RE HERE."

Tatyana opened her eyes as they entered the lot and parked near the museum.

"How long have I been asleep?"

"Over an hour."

"So much for a short nap."

She stretched her arms, loosening the kinks in her neck and shoulders. As she did, Piotr opened the rear door. Nostradamus jumped out and raced over to the closest tree. Tatyana climbed out next. Beata stood nearby.

"Welcome back, Miss Reynolds."

"It's my pleasure."

"I was so excited when Stanisław called to say you were returning today. After what happened last time, I was afraid you might not want to."

"I don't give up easily."

Finished with his business, Nostradamus wandered around the parking lot, sniffing the area. Tatyana clapped the side of her leg three times.

"Come here, boy."

He raced over, his tail wagging. Tatyana attached the leash to his harness.

Tayana gave Stanisław and Beata one bloodstone each and attached the third, which she had placed in a small leather pouch, to Nostradamus' collar. She would keep the last two for herself.

"What are these?" asked Stanisław.

"They're bloodstones, crystals that will protect you from the darkness lingering here. Keep them on you at all times."

Beata looked concerned. "Do you think we'll need them?"

"No," Tatyana lied. "But better to be safe than sorry."

Stanisław slid the stone into his pants pocket. "Thank you."

"You're welcome. I'm ready when you are."

"Follow me."

Beata led the way to the camp. Stanisław advised Piotr that they might be a few hours, then removed Tatyana's travel bag from the trunk and followed.

"Have there been any more incidents of paranormal activity since I was here last?"

"Not a one. Hopefully, we won't have to worry about it after today."

As they walked up the incline past the station platform and entered the camp, Tatyana braced herself to be overwhelmed by the trapped spirits as had happened her last time here. She only detected an intense background hum that slightly increased the farther she proceeded, as if the spirits were merely acknowledging her presence, which made sense. She already had been fully immersed in the spectral realm. Thankfully, none of the spirits of the SS officers made themselves known.

Nostradamus acted apprehensively, remembering what

happened to his mistress earlier, but his demeanor did not indicate the active presence of entities. Still, he stayed close to Tatyana.

Tatyana stopped ten yards from the monolith and took the travel bag from Stanisław. "You two wait here."

"What are you going to do?" asked Beata.

"I'm going to cleanse some of the negativity from this place before sending the spirits on their way."

"Do you need help?" asked Stanisław.

"I should be okay. I'll yell if I need you."

"Good luck."

Tatyana crouched in front of Nostradamus. "Do you want to join me?"

The dog stepped back a step and lightly whimpered. She cupped his jaw, kissed him on the snout, and handed the leash to Stanisław. She then made her way to the first set of memorial stones covering the eleven burial pits spread throughout the camp.

Nick stood in the center of the first set of stones, waiting for her. He smiled. "They're glad you're here."

"Beata was afraid I wouldn't come back."

"I'm talking about the spirits. They know you're here to help, and they appreciate it."

The comment made Tatyana feel good. She only hoped she did not disappoint them.

Placing her travel bag on the ground, Tatyana removed a lighter and a bundle of sage. She flipped on the flame and held it to the bundle. When the sage began to burn, she slid the lighter into her pocket and strolled through the memorials.

"I address myself to the purest entities of the spiritual world. By all that is good and holy, I bow in humility before you and ask that you cover me with the white light and protection of the pure spirits. I claim the protection of this light for myself, for my friends, and for those who are condemned to this location. I take a stand against all that is evil and negative."

Opening her travel bag, she removed a plate, laid it on the ground in the center of the formation, lit another bundle of sage, and placed it on the plate. Moving to the opposite end of the formation, she repeated the process.

She performed the same ritual at the other ten burial sites and the burn pit. Nick stayed by her side the entire time in case trouble brewed.

"Where did you get the plates?" asked Nick as she cleansed the last of the stone formations.

"I borrowed them from the hotel."

"You mean you stole them."

"No. I plan on returning them."

After completing the ceremonies, she felt a minor decrease in the negativity hovering over the area.

Tatyana returned to the others. She cleansed the monolith last since most of the negative energy resided there. After placing a plate with burning sage along each of its four walls, Tatyana circled around to the front and lit another bundle. A warmth of sympathy from the trapped spirits washed over her. Nick stood to her left.

"Are you ready?"

Nick nodded.

"I call out to the spirits of those tormented souls rooted to this monstrous location. I give myself to the purest entities of the spiritual world. I banish fear and anger from my own life. As shall it be with me, shall it be with this camp. I banish fear and anger from this area and cast it back to the realm of darkness where it belongs." Tatyana closed her eyes. "You are free. Please, take this opportunity to move on to the—"

The warmth Tatyana had experienced a few moments earlier burned away to be replaced by a cold, evil malevolence, a combination of anger, hatred, and self-righteousness. From behind her, Nostradamus growled menacingly. She opened her eyes and gasped.

The spirits of two men stood in front of her. They wore the

traditional grey uniforms of the SS, with silver runes on their collar tabs and the infamous skull and crossbones on their officer caps. Each stood at least six feet tall. Their blue eyes glared at her, filled with rage and loathing. The taller of the two men had a four-inch scar running down from his right cheek to his jaw. He sneered.

"We warned you to stay away, but you wouldn't listen."

"I'm not frightened by you."

"You should be." The sneer morphed into a sardonic grin. "Now, you'll pay for your arrogance."

A sharp pain erupted across Tatyana's back, momentarily blurring her vision. Before she could recover, two more jolts crisscrossed her shoulders, the pain so intense she fell to her knees. She turned slightly to her right. A third SS officer stood behind her, brandishing a whip made of intertwined rope, a malicious expression on his face. He brought it down a fourth time, the tip connecting with her neck and left cheek. Welts formed where each blow struck.

"You bastard!" Nick lunged at the officer holding the whip.

The second SS officer blocked his path, his spiritual energy holding Nick in place. He studied Nick for a moment and laughed sardonically.

"You wear the naval uniform of our enemy. How does it feel to be helpless?"

Nick wanted to retort, but every part of him was frozen.

Nostradamus broke free from Stanisław and raced to help his mistress, his lips curled over his teeth, his ears down against his skull. The dog lunged at the SS officer with the whip.

The spirits of a German Shepherd and an Alsatian guard dog materialized out of nowhere and pounced on Nostradamus, knocking him to the ground. Nostradamus fought back, but despite his size and strength, he was no match for the other two dogs. The Shepherd kept Nostradamus pinned to the ground while the Alsatian went after his throat. Nostradamus bit at both dogs, futilely attempting to keep them at bay.

The officer with the whip grinned and lashed Tatyana two more times. Despite her best efforts, she screamed in pain.

"I'll kill you!" Nick tried to lunge at the officer holding him in place but could not break the spiritual hold.

The second officer withdrew his Luger and aimed it at Nick's head.

"I'm dead, asshole. You can't kill me."

The officer raised the pistol and brought it down across Nick's face. Nick tried to punch him but could not move. The guard continued to pummel Nick's face with the stock of the Luger.

The tall SS officer motioned for the third one to stop the whipping. He stepped forward and crouched before Tatyana.

"You were warned not to interfere, and you didn't listen. Everything that happens now is your fault."

He stood and nodded. The officer with the whip resumed his attack, viciously bringing the thick ropes down on her back. The agony became unbearable. Tatyana clenched her teeth and silently absorbed each blow, refusing to give in to the Nazis.

Nostradamus yelped. Tatyana looked over, terrified. The Alsatian had sunk its teeth into her dog's shoulder and was shaking its head back and forth. Blood flowed from the wounds. Nostradamus whimpered. Despite the pain, he still attempted to fight off the two guard dogs.

Tears flowed down Tatyana's face. The realization suddenly set in. Nick had tried to warn her, yet she refused to listen. Her overconfidence had gotten in the way of common sense. The earlier dealing with Kathleen, Eliza Adams, and Dr. Savage had given her a false sense that she could easily handle this situation. Only she had greatly miscalculated the evil inherent in the Nazis and their total disdain for human life. And now the two most important people in her life were paying for her pride. Tatyana had to end this before Nostradamus died.

"Alright, I'll go!"

The tall SS officer gestured for the whipping to stop and crouched in front of Tatyana again.

"Are you surrendering?"

"Yes," Tatyana whimpered.

"Say it."

"Please, don't make me."

"Say it!"

Nostradamus cried out. Tatyana's heart ached.

"I surrender. Just call off your dogs."

The tall SS officer whistled. The two dogs ceased their attack and backed away, looking to their master for further orders. Nostradamus went limp, panting heavily.

The tall SS officer leaned closer to Tatyana, placed his hand against her chin, and lifted her head so she had to meet his gaze. His face bore a vindictive smile of victory, making the scar even more pronounced. He spoke in a low, menacing voice.

"If you show up here again, we will kill all of you. You will watch us torture to death your dog, your spirit companion, and any human you bring along. Once your will is broken, we will kill you, brutally, slowly. You will die in agony and with the knowledge that you're responsible for the suffering the others endured."

The tall SS officer stood and moved back a step. He bellowed an order in German, and he and the other spirits dissolved into a mist that quickly dissipated.

Tatyana ran over to Nostradamus and knelt beside him. Blood flowed from bite marks on his right shoulder. She petted his head. On feeling her touch, Nostradamus wagged his tail.

Nick knelt beside Tatyana. "Are you okay?"

"Screw that. I'm worried about Nostradamus."

Stanisław and Beata raced up a few seconds later. The woman stayed a few feet to the rear. Stanisław knelt beside Tatyana, examining her back.

"We need to get you to a hospital."

Tatyana shook her head. "We need to get Nostradamus to the vet first."

"But you're bleeding."

"I don't care!" Tatyana looked over at Stanisław, her eyes pleading.

"Okay, Wait here." Stanisław stood. "Beata, keep an eye on them. I'm going to get the car."

CHAPTER THIRTEEN

THEY FOUND A pet hospital in the nearby town of Brok. Dr. Chlebek, the vet on duty, rushed Nostradamus into the emergency room, leaving a crying Tatyana in the waiting area. Nick sat beside her, saying nothing, merely being there for support.

Stanisław stood nearby. "Are you okay?"

"I'm worried about my dog."

"They'll take good care of him. I promise."

"Thanks."

Stanisław stepped over to the counter, flashed the woman his credentials, and spoke with her for a minute in Polish. She nodded and called someone over the speaker system.

Stanisław came back over. "We're going into Exam Room One."

"What for?"

"One of the vet techs is going to check your wounds."

"I'm not a dog." Her attempt at humor fell flat.

"I want someone to look at your wounds since you refuse to go to the ER. You're bleeding badly."

Tatyana had tampered down her own physical suffering, concentrating instead on Nostradamus. Now that he was being taken care of, she again became aware of the intense pain in her back. It was so bad she could barely stand. Stanisław guided her into the exam room. Nick joined them.

Tatyana sat in one of the chairs. Stanisław and Nick stood against the wall, both men concerned about her well-being.

"I can't believe what happened back there," said Stanisław.

"Those were actual SS officers."

"You saw them?"

"Their spirits, yes. Beata and I tried to help you but were frozen in place. We couldn't move. Sorry."

"No need to apologize. It wasn't your fault. The spirit world is capable of a lot of things." Tatyana glanced up at him. "I'm sorry I gave up."

"Sorry? I can't believe you endured what you did for so long."

Someone knocked on the door. Stanisław said something in Polish, and then a young female tech vet entered. The two conversed for a minute, and then Stanisław turned his attention back to Tatyana.

"This is Katarzyna. She wants you to take off your shirt and bra and sit backward in the chair so she can treat your wounds."

Tatyana unbuttoned her blouse, nearly screaming from the agony caused by the act. Stanisław positioned himself facing the wall with his back to her.

Nick still leaned against the wall, smiling.

"Turn around."

"I am," said Stanisław.

Nick chuckled. "It's not like I haven't seen you naked before."

The disapproving glare Tatyana flashed him made Nick face away rather than incur her wrath.

Some of the blood had started to dry, adhering part of the shirt to her skin. As each section tore loose, it sent an ache through her body. Once the shirt had been removed, Katarzyna undid Tatyana's bra strap and examined the wounds. Katarzyna and Stanisław spoke for a few minutes in Polish.

"You have eleven lacerations," said Stanisław. "Katarzyna is going to clean them with alcohol, stitch them closed, and cover them with bandages."

"In other words, this is going to be painful."

"Incredibly so. Unfortunately, they have nothing to give you for the pain. You need to go to the ER."

"I'll go later. I'm not leaving Nostradamus alone. Tell her to go ahead."

Stanisław spoke to Katarzyna, who nodded and began removing the necessary supplies from the cabinets, placing them on a mayo tray. She unwrapped two hypodermic needles from their protective coverings and filled them with a clear liquid from two vials.

"What are those for?"

Stanisław questioned the nurse, who turned to Tatyana and answered in heavily accented English. "Lidocaine. Deaden feeling in shoulders."

Katarzyna moved behind Tatyana and carefully injected the lidocaine into the skin around the lacerations. When the last of the injections had been completed, she disposed of the hypodermics into a biohazard bin, then arranged the instruments on the mayo tray as she waited for the medication to take effect. After several minutes, the vet tech wiped down the first laceration with alcohol wipes. Tatyana winced. The pain was nowhere near as intense as when they first arrived, but the discomfort from cleaning the wounds drove her crazy.

"Beata and I saw what happened but didn't hear what the Germans said to you," said Stanisław. "Do you mind filling me in?"

"Now?"

"It'll take your mind off of things."

Tatyana could not argue with that. Maybe relating what had taken place would distract her. She relayed what had transpired between her and the tall SS officer. She completed her story at the same time Katarzyna finished cleaning the wounds and began stitching the lacerations. Compared to the aggravation from being doused in alcohol, the needle piercing her skin seemed like nothing.

"I'm sorry you had to go through all this," said Stanisław. "My government will have to find some other way to cleanse those ghosts."

"What are you talking about?" Tatyana turned toward him, sending a bolt of pain down her back.

Katarzyna chastised her in Polish.

"She told you to stay still. I don't expect you to stay on this case after what happened today."

"Damn it, Tatyana," blurted Nick. "Don't you realize what you're dealing with?"

"I do, but I'm not backing down."

Stanisław shook his head. "I can't let you put your life at risk again."

"It's not your decision to make. It's mine. And I'm seeing this through."

"Are you sure?"

"Yes. You can't appease evil. Evil must be eliminated."

"Thank you." Stanisław's voice had a grateful tone. "How are you going to do it?"

"I haven't figured out that part yet."

No one spoke for the rest of the procedure. Katarzyna quickly sutured the remaining lacerations, covered them with bandages, and then spoke to Stanisław.

"Katarzyna says you can put your shirt back on, but she recommends ditching your bra until you see a doctor."

"Tell her thanks."

Stanisław thanked Katarzyna in Polish before she departed. Tatyana slid off her bra, gently pulled on her blood-soaked shirt, and buttoned it up.

"You can turn around now."

"How do you feel?" asked Stanisław.

"It hurts, but I'll live. I can use some pain meds, though."

"We'll get you some on the way—"

Dr. Chlebek entered and conversed with Stanisław.

"Nostradamus is fine. The bite was deep, but nothing major was damaged. It'll take a few weeks to heal completely, and he'll be in ache for the next few days, but there should be no permanent injuries. They gave him a rabies shot, some antibiotics, and some pain meds. There's a supply of the latter two waiting at the front desk for him when we leave. He should wake up from the anesthesia soon. He'll be groggy for a day or two but will be well enough to take home."

"Tell the veterinarian thank you from me, please."

Stanisław relayed the message. Dr. Chlebek smiled and responded in broken English, "You're welcome."

When the vet departed, Tatyana asked, "How much do I owe them?"

"Nothing. All the medical bills will be taken care of by my government. It's the least we can do. We'll wait in the car until Nostradamus is ready. You can rest there."

"I'll see you back at the hotel," said Nick before disappearing into a mist.

Once in the car, Tatyana reclined the front seat. Considering the discomfort in her back, she doubted she would be able to rest, but surprisingly, she dozed off after a few minutes.

CHAPTER FOURTEEN

NOSTRADAMUS HAD BEEN happy to see his mistress when released from the vet hospital, though he was so drugged up he could barely stand. Still, he refused to be left behind when they reached the emergency room in Warsaw, sitting patiently with her in the waiting area before dozing off. Stanisław stayed with him while the nurses checked out Tatyana.

The attending nurse spoke English. She told Tatyana that the vet techs had done an excellent job stitching her wounds, then gave her twin injections, one an antibiotic and the other the painkiller Algocalmin. The nurse made a lame joke about not having a treat to give her. She wrote an oral prescription for the two drugs to take for a week and sent Tatyana home.

When they pulled up in front of the hotel, Piotr parked at the end of the drop-off area and shut down the engine.

"You don't have to bother seeing me in," said Tatyana, embarrassed by her situation. "I'll be fine."

"It's not a bother. Considering you're on pain meds, I'd be remiss if I didn't escort you to your room. Besides...." Stanisław exited the passenger side, opened the trunk, and removed her travel bag. "You'll need help carrying this."

Tatyana relented. She climbed out. Nostradamus did not budge an inch. She pulled on the leash, but the dog stayed on the seat, his eyes open and glazed over. She would have her hands full getting the dog upstairs. Piotr noticed and helped her, lifting Nostradamus out of the back seat and onto the sidewalk, taking the leash, and leading him into the hotel, occasionally raising the dog back on his feet when he laid down to nap.

When they reached Tatyana's room, Stanisław placed her travel bag on the coffee table. Piotr unfastened the harness around Nostradamus and put it on the small table by the front door. He petted the dog and left.

"Do you need anything before I go?" asked Stanisław.

"You've already done more than enough. Thank you."

"*Nie ma za co.*" Stanisław made his way to the door, then paused and faced Tatyana. "Considering what happened today, are you sure you want to continue with this? My government would understand if you wanted to head back to the States. After what I witnessed today, I wouldn't blame you."

"I appreciate that, but I'm seeing this through to the end. I refuse to let evil win."

"You're brave to stand up to the SS."

"They're only spirits, and spirits can be controlled. Today was my fault. I was overconfident and allowed them to get the better of me. Next time will be different." Tatyana spoke the last sentence with more enthusiasm than she felt.

"Let me know what you need, and my government will make sure you have it."

"All I need is a few days to gather my thoughts and come up with a plan of action."

"Take all the time necessary. Goodnight."

Tatyana saw Stanisław to the door and locked it after he left. When she entered the suite, Nick sat at his usual spot on the sofa, urging Nostradamus to join him. The dog wanted to but did not have the energy. He stared at Nick, his eyelids drooping and his front paws slowly sliding to each side. Giving up, Nostradamus laid down on the carpet and immediately fell asleep. Tatyana entered the bedroom, removed a blanket from the closet, returned to the suite, and covered her beloved pet.

"How are you feeling?" asked Nick.

Tatyana slid off her shoes and dropped into the love seat. "I'm exhausted."

"That's the painkillers. But I was referring to your back."

"It hurts like Hell. And I know tomorrow it'll be even worse." Tatyana stretched. The lacerations ached. "How are you feeling? I watched that officer beat you up with his Luger."

"I have no corporeal form, so I didn't feel anything. The son of a bitch should have known that, but he was arrogant. He enjoyed the act of being violent."

An uneasy silence passed between them before Nick spoke again.

"I'm sorry I wasn't of more help."

"You tried, but they overpowered you. And when those dogs attacked Nostradamus…." Her heart ached over what she had put the poor thing through.

"The SS harnessed the dark energy of the camp against you."

"But I had cleansed the camp of the dark energy before I began."

"Your senses were overwhelmed by the tortured souls of the prisoners, so I doubt you detected it. The ground itself has a dark energy about it, much greater than you originally sensed, which is understandable given what happened there. I picked up on it while you were conducting your cleansing ritual." Nick leaned forward and rested his arms on his knees. "The SS harnesses that energy to increase their power. When they do, they become unstoppable."

"That explains how three spirits can keep nine hundred thousand at bay."

"Exactly. It's how they were able to immobilize me, Stanisław, and Beata. Even worse, they only used a fraction of the darkness. If they had used it all, I doubt any of us would have survived."

"Why did they go so easy on us?"

"My impression is they're trying to scare us off."

Tatyana sighed. "It worked."

"It also means the next time we deal with them, the SS will come after us with everything they have. Considering how much dark energy exists in the camp, we're going to face an evil we've never encountered before."

"Does that scare you?"

"Yes."

The fact Nick was scared lessened her optimism.

Tatyana leaned back into the loveseat, moaning when her back touched the leather. "You warned me before. I'm way in over my head."

"To be honest, yes, you are. But I'm proud of you for standing up to them the way you did. That took a lot of courage."

Coming from a man who faced numerous *kamikaze* attacks meant a lot. "I still folded like a house of cards when they went after Nostradamus."

"That's how those assholes operate. They wear away at your morale until it breaks, then you have no choice but to give in. All we need to do is figure out how to get the better of them."

Tatyana forced a grin. "Easier said than done."

"True. But if anyone can figure this out, it'll be you. I have faith in you."

Nick's words soothed her shattered spirits.

"Don't worry about it now." Nick reached out a hand and placed it in Tatyana's. The positive energy felt good. "You need to take care of yourself and Nostradamus. You both went through a lot today. Rest up tonight and worry about it in the morning."

"Is that an order?"

"Like you'd ever take orders from me." Nick chuckled. "Consider it advice from a friend."

"Don't worry. I will."

"Good. Call me when you need me."

Nick stood and disappeared with his usual fanfare, hoping it would make his friend feel comfortable. It did.

Tatyana crawled onto the floor, snuggled beside Nostradamus, pulled half the blanket over herself, and joined her pet in a long sleep.

CHAPTER FIFTEEN

TATYANA WOKE UP mid-morning restless and aching. Her dreams had once again been haunted by the nightmare events that constantly played out in her mind. Nostradamus was already awake and feeling much better, giving his mistress a face bath when she opened her eyes.

She spent the next two days relaxing and allowing the wounds to heal. The pain wasn't as annoying as her frustration over not being able to come up with an idea for cleansing Treblinka of the dark energy and the SS and freeing the tormented souls from their imprisonment.

Tatyana's back felt better on the morning of the third day, though every movement pulled at the stitches, causing her constant discomfort. But she needed to get her ass in gear. After buying a sweatshirt in the gift shop one size too big to help ease the tenderness, she took Nostradamus for a long walk. They both needed the exercise and time to clear their heads.

As she entered the lobby, Stanisław stood at the concierge desk with a phone in his hand. On seeing Tatyana, he hung up and approached.

"I was calling your room to see if you were here."

"I was taking Nostradamus for a walk."

"That's fine. I'm sorry to drop in on you unannounced, but I have something you need to see." He held up a sealed manila folder.

"Come on up."

Once in the suite, Stanisław sat in the loveseat as Tatyana removed Nostradamus' harness and scratched his head. She stepped over to the minibar and removed a bottle of water.

"Do you want anything?"

"A bottle of water, if you have one."

Tatyana grabbed a second bottle, closed the minibar, and sat on the sofa. She placed the bottle in front of Stanisław.

"Thank you."

"No problem. Your government is paying for it."

Stanisław was so excited about the information that the joke went over his head. He pushed the envelope across the coffee table. "Take a look at this."

"What is it?"

"The names of the three SS officers killed during the revolt at Treblinka."

"How did you find them?"

"I had two of my men do a deep dive to see if the names were recorded anywhere. We have Nazi documents in our archives left behind when the Soviets pushed out the Germans. Among them was the diary of a former SS guard who served at Treblinka. He was there when the breakout occurred and wrote about it afterward, including the names of the officers who were killed. Once we had the names, we were able to pull their records." Stanisław pointed to the envelope. "Those are their photos."

Tatyana opened the envelope and removed three 8x10 photographs. The first image sent a cold chill down her spine.

It showed three SS officers standing by the door to the crematorium, watching a stream of Jews as they filed to their deaths. The two on the ends did not look familiar, but the tall one in the center did, and scared her. He stood well over six feet tall and smiled. Not a smile of pleasantry, but of sadistic enjoyment that those in front of him would soon be gassed. What stood out most was the scar that ran down his right cheek from the corner of his eye to the jaw.

"That's the officer who threatened me."

"That's what I thought. He's *Standartenführer* Reinhard

Mueller, one of the most vicious guards at Treblinka. He oversaw the gassing of new arrivals from the trains. If the crowd became unsettled, he would scare them into submission by taking the youngest child from its mother, grabbing it by the legs, and smashing its head against the crematorium. Years after the war, he was tried in absentia by a war crimes commission and sentenced to death by hanging."

"Did he get the scar during the revolt?"

Stanisław shook his head. "Mueller took fencing in college. He got that scar during a duel with Reinhard Heydrich."

"Who's that?"

"Himmler's second in command and the one who orchestrated the Final Solution. The two became friends after the duel. Mueller boasted about their friendship to anyone who would listen."

Tatyana swallowed the bile rising in her throat and moved to the second photo. It was the official photograph of a man in his late twenties, with blonde hair and blue eyes filled with pride.

"That's the officer who whipped me."

"It makes sense. He's *Obersturmführer* Hans Todt. He was known for abusively whipping prisoners who got out of line. Several died on the spot from the punishment he inflicted. According to the diary, several prisoners who had been beaten by Todt sought him out during the revolt and beat him to death with his whip."

"Serves the bastard right." It explained the ferocity of the whipping he had inflicted on her. He was out for revenge.

Tatyana moved to the third photograph. It must have been taken during a break in the killings. It showed an SS officer seated on a bench, his arms stretched out along the backrest, a cigarette in his right hand. He was laughing with a fellow officer who stood in front of the bench as if they were enjoying a day at the beach rather than the destruction of an entire ethnic group.

"Does he look familiar?" asked Stanisław.

"That's the officer who held everyone in place."

"He's *Untersturmführer* Josef Heinz. One of the SS assigned to the fake hospital. Heinz would help execute any infirm prisoners brought there and toss the bodies into a ditch."

Tatyana dropped the photos onto the coffee table and closed her eyes, trying to force from her mind the terrifying images she experienced on that first day.

"It's hard to believe people as evil as this existed."

"Sadly, it's a reality," Stanisław replied. "Our inhumanity to others is the only constant in history."

Tatyana could not argue. She had experienced more than her fair share of such brutality since becoming a paranormal investigator, though never on such a massive scale.

"Does it help knowing who those SS officers are?"

"More than you can imagine. I now have a slight advantage. Not only do I know what to expect from them, but they've been using their anonymity against me. They can't hide behind it anymore. Tell your men they did a fantastic job researching this."

"They'll be happy to hear they were a help."

"Can your people get me more information specific to them?"

"I don't know, but I'll ask them to keep digging." Stanisław stood. "I don't want to take up any more of your time. Return those photos when you're done and call me when you're ready to go back. I'll see myself out."

After Stanisław left, Tatyana studied the three photos for a few minutes before slipping them back into the envelope. She spent the next hour trying to figure out a way to defeat the SS and the dark energy holding the tormented souls of Treblinka at bay, but with no success. Every idea she came up with had several cons attached, making them too risky. Her next confrontation would be all or nothing, so she had to do this right. Her life literally depended on it.

Frustrated and aching, Tatyana decided that some painkillers and a nap would be the best thing for her. This time, the pills allowed her to get a much-needed rest. Even so, she woke up with no solution to her predicament.

She decided to return to the metaphysical shop in the Mokotów District, hoping something there might spur her imagination.

CHAPTER SIXTEEN

T HE CONCIERGE CALLED a cab for Tatyana and gave the driver the address with instructions to wait and return her to the hotel. She gave the concierge a generous tip and used the drive to clear her head. God knows she needed to be clear-minded when discussing her options with the shopkeeper.

On entering the store, Tatyana's senses were greeted with the pleasantly familiar scent of burning sage. She inhaled deeply. Her spirit immediately felt better. She decided to buy some more to cleanse her suite of any lingering darkness.

"*Czy mogę ci pomóc?*"

The question came from an elderly lady who emerged from the back room. She was short, barely five feet in height, with her hunched over back making her appear even tinier. The woman had a wrinkled face that indicated a life of hardship and white, unkempt hair. Tatyana guessed the woman to be in her mid- to late eighties. She wore traditional Polish clothes rather than anything modern—a long, red, pleated dress, a white blouse, and a black, sleeveless vest with embroidered flowers. The garments were old and slightly worn but still in good condition.

"I'm sorry. I don't speak Polish."

"I asked if I could be of any help," the woman said in slightly accented English. "I'm Danuta. I own this place."

"I'm just browsing for now." She approached the counter and offered her hand. "I'm Tatyana."

Danuta shook the hand but did not let go, staring at Tatyana warily. "You're the American who was here three days ago. My granddaughter told me about you. She said you had an evil aura around you but did not mention how intense it was."

"I've been through a lot the past twenty-four hours."

"I can tell." Danuta clutched Tatyana's hand, studying her. "The aura doesn't emanate from you but hangs around you, waiting for an opportunity to darken your soul. It's highly malicious and powerful."

"That's one of the reasons I'm here. To cleanse myself."

"It won't be easy." Danuta released her hand. "You picked this up at Treblinka?"

"How did you know?"

"My granddaughter. She was concerned for your safety. You scared her." Danuta made her way along the back of the counter to the set of antique winged-back chairs in the corner. "I wish I was here at the time. I would have warned you against going there."

"I had no choice."

"We all have a choice, dear." Danuta sat in one of the chairs and motioned to the empty one. "Tell me what happened."

Tatyana sat down and relayed what had transpired over the last few weeks, from the deaths of the neo-Nazis to the encounter two days ago with the spirits of the SS. Danuta met her gaze the entire time, expressing no emotions. When Tatyana finished, the elderly woman shook her head.

"When I heard what happened to those three teenagers, I was afraid something like this would occur. All the former camps are awash with darkness waiting to be released. Those were terrible days."

"Were you there?"

"Not in the camps, but I was alive during that time."

"You don't look that old."

Danuta smiled. "You're sweet. I'm ninety-three. I was a young girl during the Holocaust. And I'm Jewish. My family died in Auschwitz early in the war. I survived only because the family of a Christian friend of mine took me in. She told the authorities I was a cousin from eastern Poland displaced by the Soviets when they occupied the region in 1939."

"That was nice of them."

"It was foolish. If the Nazis ever found out, the entire family would have been sent to a camp. Standing up to evil is dangerous. But you know that."

Tatyana lowered her head.

Danuta leaned forward and patted Tatyana's hand. "You should be proud of yourself. Not many people show your type of courage. If more people had, the Holocaust might never have happened."

"Thank you. I'm just at a loss about how to deal with this situation."

"The answer is right in front of you, dear."

The statement caught Tatyana by surprise. "I don't understand."

"The Nazis were at their strongest when they inspired fear amongst those around them. It was their source of power. It's how they kept the German people in line and got millions of them to march to their deaths. The Nazis had no idea how to deal with resistance, and it terrified them."

"How so?"

"Look how they dealt with any German who resisted National Socialism. The 20 July plotters. The White Rose Society. They brutally murdered anyone who stood up to them to terrorize the others into submission. The same thing happened in Warsaw in 1944 when the Jewish ghetto rose up and fought back. It took several days for the Nazis to regain their composure. When they finally invaded the ghetto, they executed every man, woman, and child they came across and sent those who surrendered to camps." Danuta paused. "Why didn't they do the same thing to you at Treblinka?"

"They did," Tatyana protested. "One of the SS officers

whipped me eleven times, and their dogs almost killed Nostra-damus."

"And when you begged them to stop, they agreed without conditions?"

"No." Tatyana tried to hide her frustration. "The SS officer let me go on condition that I never go back."

Danuta leaned forward and spoke softly. "Because they're scared of you."

"Why would the SS be scared of me?"

Danuta pointed a finger at Tatyana and sat back in her seat. "That's a question only you can answer. There's some-thing different about you I've never sensed from other investigators. I pick up on it but can't put my finger on it. It might be a special connection you have with the spirit realm. It might be an untapped power. Personally, I think it's a courage you have inside you that terrifies those Nazi spirits."

"No." Tatyana shook her head. "I willingly gave in to them and agreed never to return."

"When they attacked you, or when they went after your loved one?"

The realization dawned on Tatyana.

"And you're going back, aren't you? That's why you're here."

"Yes."

"Then you need to fully understand the extent of the evil you face. You must talk with Greta."

Tatyana was confused. "Who's Greta?"

"Someone who experienced the evil first-hand."

"A camp survivor?"

"Worse." Before Tatyana could continue the conversation, Danuta asked, "Where are you staying?"

"The Warsaw Marriott."

"I'll have her call you in the next few days."

Danuta smiled and slowly stood, wavering a little. Tatyana helped her up. The elderly woman tapped Tatyana's hand as a gesture of thanks.

"Don't overthink this, dear. You're questioning your abilities and how you reacted. The spirits of all those trapped there believe in you. It's why they reached out to you. And so do the SS officers, which is why they're trying to scare you off. Once you talk to Greta, you'll have a better understanding of what you face. Listen to the spirits of those trapped there. They'll guide you and show you how to defeat evil. Now, if you'll excuse me."

Shuffling past Tatyana, Danuta made her way toward the back room. "An old woman like me has to rest. Take your time and figure out a way to stop them. When you do, come back and I'll set you up with what you need. I'll also have something special for you."

"I don't know if I can handle this."

"You can, dear. Just have faith in yourself." Danuta paused and nodded toward Tatyana. "I do."

The elderly woman entered the back room, letting the curtains close behind her.

Tatyana headed outside and got into the taxi, which returned her to the hotel. She sat in the back seat, staring out the window at the city as it passed, but did not notice it. Her thoughts centered around Danuta's advice to outsmart the SS. It was possible. She only needed to figure out how. Tatyana tried to convince herself she could do it.

She had to.

She could not let Danuta down.

Nor could she let down the myriad of tormented souls trapped at Treblinka.

CHAPTER SEVENTEEN

T ATYANA SPENT THE rest of the day and the next morning contemplating what Danuta had said about utilizing the fear of the SS to defeat them.

Easier said than done.

On the plus side, Nostradamus seemed more like his usual self. She ordered a steak entrée from room service for her lunch, and he stood by the table, licking his lips and giving her the mooch eyes. Needless to say, he got several pieces.

Tatyana finished her lunch when the phone rang. She picked it up on the fourth ring.

"Is this Miss Reynolds?"

"It is."

"This is the concierge. There is someone in the lobby who says you're expecting her. The woman's name is Greta."

Tatyana was taken aback. She had expected Greta to call ahead and arrange the meeting, but beggars can't be choosers.

"Tell her I'll be right down."

A muffled conversation ensued, then the concierge said, "Greta says to take your time. She'll meet you in the bar."

Five minutes later, Tatyana entered the lobby. The concierge walked her to the bar and motioned to a booth in the far corner. "That's Greta."

"Thank you."

As she made her way across the room, Tatyana was surprised to see a woman almost as old as Danuta seated in the booth. Unlike Danuta, whose face showed decades of hardship, this woman had aged with elegance, though that most likely was from her being financially well off. A fur coat lay folded beside her. She wore a tan, satin blouse adorned with expensive jewelry. Her hair was well-coiffured, and it looked as though she recently had a manicure. Yet it was the woman's countenance that threw off Tatyana. She had a confidence usually reserved for people who had led a rich life but with an underlying tone of depression. Not so much depression as shame.

"Are you Greta?"

"I am." She motioned to the seat opposite her. "Please join me, Miss Reynolds."

"You can call me Tatyana."

Greta held up her tumbler. "Would you like some whiskey?"

"I'm fine, thank you."

Greta downed half the tumbler in one gulp. "Danuta tells me you're trying to free the souls of those who died at Treblinka, but the spirits of SS officers are fighting you. Is that true?"

"Yes."

"I admire your courage."

"I wouldn't call it courage. They scared me off the last time. One of the spirits whipped me eleven times, and they almost killed my dog. I agreed to stop what I was doing if they let him go."

"Danuta says you're going back to try again."

"I am."

"That, my dear, is a courage few people showed during the Third Reich."

Tatyana waited for Greta to continue, but the woman remained silent.

"Danuta says you have insights into the evils of the SS that might help in dealing with them."

"I do." Greta closed her eyes and finished the tumbler, then called the bartender for a refill. Tatyana waited for the bartender to bring the drink before resuming.

"Were you a victim of the SS like Danuta?"

"A victim, yes. But not like Danuta. She's such a lovely person for letting me be her friend."

"I don't understand."

Greta took a deep breath. "I was the daughter of an SS guard at Auschwitz."

Tatyana was stunned. It took several seconds before she could speak again.

"Did you know what your father did for a living?'

"Yes. I was only seven at the time, and I didn't know all the details until after the war, but I knew he worked at the camp."

"He told you where he worked?"

"He didn't have to." Greta took another swig of whiskey. "We lived beside the camp."

"Near it?"

"*Beside* it. Our backyard bordered the stone wall that surrounded the compound. My friends and I would go down to the tracks and watch the trains enter, although at the time we didn't know what… who was in them. My first winter there, I thought the snow in Poland was black. Only much later did I find out that it was the ashes of those cremated that exited the smokestacks. That's how close we lived."

Tatyana had no idea how to respond.

"Like most fathers, mine never discussed what he did at work. At home, he was the perfect father. At least, it seemed that way to a seven-year-old who, at the time, didn't know any better. He never raised his voice to me or my mother or hit us. When he got home, he would hug me and ask how my day was. After dinner, we played for a while, and then he read me bedtime stories before I went to sleep. He was a good father and a faithful husband. He even got me a cat to play with. We would have birthday parties, play outside, go for bike rides, laugh… everything a normal family would do. He cared deeply about us. When the Russians approached, he arranged for us to leave Poland and move to a small village in Bavaria where we would be safe.

"My father was later captured by the British and charged

with crimes against humanity. I was nine at the time and refused to believe the charges were legitimate. I assumed it was the victors taking revenge on the defeated. My mother complained that it was unfair, that my father was just perform-ing his job, and I believed her. For years, I hated the Allies for their cruelty. It wasn't until I was in my twenties that I learned the truth and have lived in shame ever since."

"Did your mother know?"

Greta nodded. "She didn't care. To her, he was merely doing his job and providing for his family. It wasn't until years later that I confronted her. She admitted to knowing what went on but claimed he did it for the good of the Reich and that I should be proud of him. We never spoke again after that." Greta averted her gaze from Tatyana. "I didn't attend her funeral."

"How do you feel about him?"

"I'm horrified." Greta finished the tumbler. "The man was a monster, a mass murderer."

"That's why you're ashamed?"

"No. I'm ashamed because I remember him as a loving, caring man who doted on his family at night rather than as the man who murdered hundreds of other families by day." Greta paused. "You must think of me as an awful person."

"I don't know what to think."

"I was an anomaly. Most of my friends were proud of their fathers' work. Even though I was disgusted by what he did as an SS officer, I still remember him as a kind-hearted, affection-ate man who loved me deeply. When I turned twenty-five, I changed my last name, broke all ties with my family and friends, and moved to Switzerland. Eventually, I married a rich banker. We had a lovely life together, though we never discussed my past. When he died several years ago, I moved back to Poland. To me, this is my home, not Germany."

Tatyana was aghast. While a part of her could understand a young girl's love for her father, she felt appalled that Greta could not hate the man for the atrocities he had committed.

"I know you don't think highly of me."

"That's not true," Tayana lied.

"It is. Don't worry. I don't think highly of myself. But that's why Danuta asked me to talk to you, to explain the evil you face." Greta leaned forward and lowered her voice. "That's the difference between the Nazis and everyone else. The communists, especially Stalin and Mao, and all the other dictators, were uneducated thugs who appealed to the worst of society. The Nazi leadership were thugs, but most of them were highly educated and came from middle-class backgrounds, and they appealed to that segment of society, people who, under normal circumstances, would never consider harming someone. Yet thousands of people, people like my father who were loving and caring fathers and husbands, committed the most barbarous atrocities without a second thought. You're not dealing with typical evil, with an evil that knows what it is and doesn't care, but with an evil composed of basically decent people who convinced themselves that what they did, the crimes against humanity they took part in, were part of the greater good."

"I don't know if I buy that."

"Read the transcripts of the Nuremberg Trials or the testimonies of Rudolf Hoess and Adolf Eichmann. They never regretted what they did. They were proud of it, and even boasted about it to their captors. An evil like that is far worse than anything we have dealt with in the recent past. If you're going to defeat it, and I hope to God you do, you must understand what you're facing."

Before Tatyana could respond, Greta stood, slipped on her fur coat, and placed a hand on Tatyana's. "I wish you the best of luck. You're going to need it."

Greta went to the bar, paid her tab, and left.

Tatyana spent the next half hour sitting in the booth, replaying everything Greta had told her. The realization slowly dawned on her that she might, in fact, be in this way over her head.

CHAPTER EIGHTEEN

ATYANA EVENTUALLY RETURNED to her suite, still disturbed by her conversation with Greta. Nick sat on the sofa, ready for his nightly visit.

"I hope I'm not disturbing you?"

"Would it matter?" she answered sarcastically as she sat on the loveseat. Deep down, she enjoyed his company and appreciated his help, especially on tough cases like this.

Nick slid into the loveseat beside her. Nostradamus curled up by his feet.

"I've been thinking about how we can stop the SS."

"Any ideas?" asked Tatyana.

Nick shook his head. "I was hoping you had better luck."

"Not really. I went back to visit that paranormal shop. The owner was an old Jewish woman who lived through the Holocaust. She arranged a meeting with a woman named Greta, who was a family member of an SS guard at Auschwitz."

"I overheard your conversation with her."

"Eavesdropping again?"

"Keeping up to date on what's going on." Nick paused. "She's right, you know."

"Greta?"

Nick nodded. "We're facing a type of evil beyond what we're used to. Did the store owner have any other ideas?"

"She thinks the SS officers are scared of me, which is why they're trying to frighten me off."

Nick thought about what she said for a moment. "Don't

take this the wrong way, but why are they afraid of you?"

"They sense I have the ability to break their hold on the camp and release the other spirits."

"You've pulled us out of situations I never thought you could, so she's probably right. Have you figured out a way to do that?"

"Nothing feasible. The only way to break their hold is to cleanse the camp of its dark energy, which would diminish their power. Then I might be able to free the other spirits."

"But the minute you try that, the SS will interfere, so you're back to square one."

"Exactly. And this time, they'll come after us with everything they have. That's the problem." Tatyana stood and paced the room. "I can't fight the SS and the dark energy of the camp at the same time."

"Too bad you can't distract the SS long enough to purge the energy and release the victims."

Tatyana stopped and ran back over to Nick. "What did you say?"

"Too bad you can't distract the SS long enough to purge the energy and release the victims."

"You're a genius." Tatyana hugged Nick, at least as much as she could considering he had no corporeal form.

"I am? I mean, of course I am."

"What would I do without you?"

"Probably live a normal life."

"We'd both be bored with that." Tatyana grabbed her jacket and headed for the door. "Keep an eye on Nostradamus until I get back."

"How long will you be?"

Tatyana did not respond. She exited the suite and went to the lobby, where she asked the concierge to hail her a taxi.

HALF AN HOUR later, Tatyana stormed into the paranormal shop, scaring Maja, who sat behind the counter.

"It's you," she said, a tone of apprehension in her voice.

"Is your grandmother here?"

Maja hesitated. "Can I help you?"

"I was here last night and chatted with your grandmother. I have to ask her a question."

"I'm sorry. She's not... available right now. If you leave your name and number—"

"It's okay, *kochany*." Danuta exited the back room, wearing the same clothes she had worn the previous evening. "I've been expecting her."

"Are you sure, grandma?"

"Yes." Danuta stepped up beside the counter and held her hand. "Please stay. I want you to be a part of this."

Maja seemed uneasy but agreed.

"I think I figured out a way to disarm the SS," Tatyana said excitedly, then laid out her plan to Danuta.

When Tatyana finished, the elderly lady smiled. "See. I told you to have faith in yourself."

"Do you think my plan will work?"

"It's the only way you'll be able to defeat such evil."

"Thank you." Tatyana could hardly conceal her excitement.

"No need to thank me, dear. I knew you'd figure it out." Danuta turned to Maja. "Help the young lady gather what she needs."

"Of course, grandma."

It took nearly an hour to assemble everything Tatyana required to perform the cleansing. The items filled two shopping bags. Once everything was gathered, Maja totaled the amount. Tatyana paid in cash.

"Will you be able to handle this alone?" asked Danuta.

"I have to. I have no one to assist me." Tatyana did not want to explain Nick.

"We can help."

"I can't ask you to put your life on the line like that."

Danuta chuckled. "Not me, dear. My days of spiritual cleansing are far behind me. I'm referring to Maja."

"Me?" Maja seemed more shocked by the offer than Tatyana.

"Yes. You have experience in the craft."

"Nothing this intense."

"Have you performed cleanings before?" asked Tatyana.

"Yes. But only ridding homes and apartments of dark energy. This is way out of my league."

"Show my granddaughter your wounds," suggested Danuta.

Both women stared at the elderly woman.

"She needs to see the extent of the evil you're dealing with."

Tatyana turned around and reluctantly lifted the back of her sweatshirt, revealing the eleven lacerations. Maja gasped. Tatyana lowered the sweatshirt.

Danuta squeezed her granddaughter's hand lovingly. "You're lucky. You were born when Poland was a democracy. You never experienced the nightmare of Nazism or Communism. This is what evil is capable of. This is what Tatyana faces. She'll need help if she's going to succeed. You're the only one who can do that."

"All I need from you is to hold things together while I perform the ritual," added Tatyana. "If it gets too dangerous, I'll let you go. I promise."

Maja glanced over at Danuta. "What do you think?"

"I know I volunteered you for this, but remember. Evil cannot be defeated unless good people confront it."

Maja caved in. "Alright, I'll go with you."

"Thank you." Tatyana looked over at Danuta. "I promise to take care of her."

"You're a kind-hearted person. I have no doubt you will.

And before you go, I have something for you."

Danuta removed a small nylon sack from her dress pocket and placed it on the counter.

"What's this?"

"A special crystals pouch. It's filled with selenite, amethyst, black obsidian, pyrite, smoky quartz, clear quartz, rainbow tourmaline, and bloodstone."

"That's a lot of protection."

"You'll need it. Most of the crystals will repel the negative energy that will come after you. The selenite will help stop the dark spirits from interfering with your energy. The clear quartz will magnify your positive energy. And the bloodstone will create a protective barrier around you and keep you safe. I also mixed in some burnt and unburnt sage to add to the cleansing effect. Take it with you while you're at Treblinka. It'll help keep you safe." Danuta glanced over to her granddaughter. "I'll make one for you tonight."

"I don't know how to thank you," said Tatyana.

"Release those spirits so they can enjoy peace in the after-life. That's the only thanks I want. And good luck."

Tatyana took her bags and left the store. She had a lot to do. First, she had to let Stanisław know she was ready to go to Treblinka and finish what she started, then let Maja know when they would pick her up. After that, she had to sort out her supplies and finalize plans.

Tomorrow would be the most challenging and dangerous day of her life.

CHAPTER NINETEEN

S TANISŁAW LEFT PIOTR behind this time and drove the car himself. He maneuvered the Mercedes around one of the many roundabouts between Warsaw and Treblinka. Once clear of the town, he switched on his high beams to better see the darkened road ahead.

"I still don't understand why you want to perform this ritual at night. Wouldn't it be easier to do it during the day?"

"Yes, but it wouldn't be as effective." Tatyana shifted in her seat to face him. "Three in the morning is when the gap between this reality and the spiritual realm is at its thinnest. It'll make it easier to communicate with the trapped spirits and urge them to move on to the afterlife."

"Doesn't it also mean it'll be that much easier for the SS to attack us?"

"It does. But once we initiate my plan, they should be neutralized long enough for me to send the others on their way."

Stanisław glanced at her. "*Should* be neutralized?"

"Nothing is guaranteed, but it's our best option." Tatyana turned to look in back. "Isn't that right, Maja?"

Maja shrugged. "If you say so."

"You and your grandmother thought the idea was good when I first laid it out to you."

"The idea is good, but I'm worried about dealing with the SS. You're much better trained than me, and look what happened to you."

For a moment, Tatyana's mind focused on the constant, dull pain across her back caused by the lacerations. This time, she had the advantage, and it would be those brutal assholes who suffered.

"We'll be fine."

"I hope so." Maja went back to silently staring out the window.

Poor Maja, thought Tatyana. The woman had not spoken since they left the metaphysical shop, spending the entire trip watching the countryside pass by and nervously massaging her hands. Not that Tatyana could blame her. Maja had never experienced anything more terrible than cleansing the homes of the few spirits trapped there, mostly those who died violently in the war and needed help to move on. She was about to face a nightmare scenario. For Maja, it would be like wading through the surf and having a *tsunami* suddenly wash ashore.

Stanisław had picked Tatyana up at the hotel at eleven. Tatyana had decided earlier to leave Nostradamus in the suite rather than bring him along. That way, the SS could not go after the dog, which would only distract Tatyana. Stanisław had been kind enough to bring along his teenage daughter to stay in the suite with Nostradamus. She hated leaving him behind, especially when he gave her that forlorn look that he might never see his mistress again.

After leaving the hotel, they swung by the metaphysical shop to pick up Maja, then headed to Treblinka. Danuta was there to wish her granddaughter good luck. Tatyana presented her plan to Danuta, who agreed she had plotted out the best option. The elderly woman gave the same pouch of crystals and sage to Stanisław and Maja, blessed the three of them, and wished them luck.

Tatyana spent the entire ride going over the details in her head, critically picking it apart, wanting to find any flaws so they were not caught off guard. She found none. The only variable was whether they could contain the SS long enough to complete their task.

Tatyana felt a spike of anxiety when Stanisław pulled off

Route 627 onto the access road leading to Treblinka. She quickly tamped it down, needing to focus on the task at hand. As they pulled into the parking lot, she checked her watch. It read 1:51.

Beata waited for them in a Volkswagen Tiguan. A man sat beside her in the driver's seat. Stanisław pulled in beside the SUV. Beata joined them.

"Who is that?" Stanisław pointed to the gentleman in the Volkswagen.

"That's my husband." She waved to him, and he waved back. "He didn't want me sitting here alone at night. But don't worry. He's staying here."

Nick materialized beside Tatayana.

"I'm glad you're here."

"I've been with you since day one. No way am I missing this."

Stanisław looked confused. "Who are you talking to?"

"Her spirit friend," Maja answered.

"Spirit friend?"

"It's time I fess up." Tatyana smiled. "I have a spirit who accompanies me on my cleansings. His name is Nick. He plays a vital role when dealing with the spiritual realm."

"He's very handsome," said Maja.

Nick laughed. "She has good taste."

Maja blushed. "Thank you."

"You can see him?" asked Stanisław.

"Yes. I also have the ability to see into the spirit realm."

Tatyana went over the plans with her team several times, having each of them repeat their roles until she was certain everyone had their part of the cleansing down pat. Their only chance of success was if everyone performed their function at the right time. When confident they were ready, Tatyana said, "Good. We all know the plan."

Nick grinned. "No plan survives first contact with the enemy."

Maja glanced over at him. "Pessimism?"

"Military wisdom."

Tatyana looked at her watch. 2:53.

"It's time. Let's do this."

The team climbed into the Mercedes. Stanisław left the parking lot and headed for the site of the death camp.

CHAPTER TWENTY

S TANISŁAW DROVE UP the incline where the train station used to exist and turned left, parking one hundred feet from the monolith. He kept the engine running and switched on the high beams.

Tatyana jumped out and removed her travel bag from the trunk. The rest of the team, including Nick, waited for her by the front of the Mercedes.

"We have to work quickly. The SS will materialize at any moment to stop us." She handed the travel bag to Maja. "Ready?"

Maja nodded.

They approached the monolith. Stanisław, Maja, and Beata broke away to the left. Tatyana and Nick continued to the monolith, stopping twenty feet before the structure. Tatyana glanced to her left. Maja and Beata were removing items from the travel bag.

"I got your back," said Nick.

Tatyana breathed deeply and took two steps forward.

"I'm back. What are you going to do about it?"

Two auras attempted to overwhelm Tatayana. One was the spirits of hundreds of thousands of tormented souls, grateful someone had the courage to free them; the other was the dark energy of the camp. Tatyana blocked them out. She now knew what to expect and how to respond.

The dark energy coalesced around Tatyana. Thanks to the crystal pouch, it could not touch Tatyana.

"Afraid to show yourselves?"

A strong wind blew across the camp, unusually cold for this time of year. Three feet from her, it formed a dust tunnel similar to a tornado and then morphed into the three SS officers. Mueller was at the forefront, with Todt and Heinz standing menacingly behind him.

Mueller sneered. "I don't know whether to admire your courage or pity your stupidity."

"You should fear me."

Mueller laughed. "Fear you?"

"I'll give you one last chance to stand aside and let me release the spirits from their imprisonment."

An expression of evil Tatyana had never seen before washed across Mueller's face. "What we did to the Jewish swine who passed through here is nothing compared to what we're about to do to you."

"Don't say I didn't warn you." Tatyana raised her right hand and snapped her fingers.

Maja and Beata rushed over. Maja used a container of salt to enclose the SS officers and Tatyana in a circle. Beata followed, placing a selenite crystal every foot along the circumference.

"What are you doing?" yelled Mueller.

"Proving you're not the master race."

When the circle was completed, Tayana backed out of its confines.

Stanisław ran up with the travel bag. Maja and Beata each removed more salt and crystals and then created a second circle around the first.

"I address myself to the purest entities of the spiritual world. I bow in humility before you and ask that you cover me with the white light and protection of the pure spirits as I walk amidst the ultimate evil. By all that is pure and holy, I claim the protection of this light for myself, for my friends, and for those tormented souls condemned to this location. As part of that protection, I ask you to limit these malevolent entities to the confines of this circle of purity and prevent them from wandering these grounds as we cleanse this area."

The dark energy spiked, trying to counter Tatyana's spell. Thunder clouds formed overhead.

"Bitch!" Mueller lunged at Tatyana, stopping when he reached the first salt circle.

When Maja and Beata finished the second circle, Tatyana backed outside of it.

"I give myself to the purest entities of the spiritual world. I refuse to show fear and back down from the darkness that haunts this place. I banish hate and anger from my own life. As shall it be with me, shall it be with this location. I banish hate and anger and cast it back to the realms of darkness where it belongs."

"Kill!" screamed Mueller.

The spirits of the German Shepperd and Alsatian materialized to Tatyana's right and rushed toward her.

Nick inserted himself between Tatyana and the guard dogs. Instinctively, they attacked the immediate threat, the Shepherd sinking its teeth into Nick's arm and the Alsatian biting his leg. As part of the spirit realm, Nick felt no pain. However, he distracted the canines long enough for Maja and Beata to form a third salt and crystal circle, enclosing the dogs.

Tatyana backed out of the third circle.

Nick suddenly dematerialized, reappearing a second later by Tatyana's side. Caught off guard, the two canines stared at each other in confusion. Their attention focused on Tatyana. They growled and attacked, being stopped by the third circle.

"I call on the purest entities of the spiritual world to keep these evil spirits at bay so I may cleanse this area of all malevolence."

Mueller's expression changed, fear replacing his anger and hatred. "Stop her!"

A fierce wind came from the trees and blew across the camp. Some of the salt within the inner circle blew away. Maja and Beata rushed up and replaced the displaced salt and crystals. Caught between the second and third circles, the two guard dogs barked and growled at the women, unable to reach them.

Mueller reached through the broken circle, clutching Maja by the hair and yanking the woman to her knees. Beata rushed over and threw salt into his face, forcing him to release Maja. As Beata refreshed the circle, Maja cited a suppression incantation in Polish. Using the local language temporarily froze the SS officers and dogs in place.

Mueller stomped his foot. "I order you to stop!"

Tatyana ignored him.

Maja and Beata retreated outside the three circles. As Maja worked on keeping the third circle intact, Stanisław and Beata removed bales of sage from the travel bag and spread out across the camp in different directions. Stanisław lit sage and dropped it around the monolith while Beata did the same to the fire pit, each time reciting a cleansing incantation Tatyana had taught them in Polish. When finished, they moved to the memorial stones and performed the same ritual.

The thunderclouds increased in intensity. A bolt of lightning shot from the sky, slamming into the monolith.

"You cannot defeat us," warned Mueller. "The darkness will prevail, and when it does, what we'll do to you and your friends is unimaginable."

Tatyana faced Mueller and smiled. "You're no match for the good that prevails."

An even more intense bolt of lightning struck the monolith. The wind grew in intensity, blowing away salt from the two inner circles. Maja's incantation had weakened, allowing the three SS officers to menacingly approach Tatyana, stopping at the third circle, which had not been broken. The two guard dogs stood on either side of them, wanting to attack the two women viciously but unable to understand why they could not reach them.

Mueller glared at Tatyana. "Once this circle is broken, I'm going to make you suffer so much you'll beg me to end your life."

Maja stopped repairing the circle and joined Tatyana. The two faced each other and held hands, combining their spiritual energy. Both women spoke an incantation simultaneously, one in Polish and the other in English.

"We take a stand against all that is evil and negative, especially the malevolent aura that shrouds this camp in its darkness. By all that is good and holy, we ask that you grant us the power to cleanse the aura and return serenity to this plot of land."

The thunder lessened in intensity, and the dark clouds thinned. Wind continued to rush across the camp, blowing salt away from the outer circle, though not as quickly as before.

"In the name of the purest entities of the spiritual world, we command the darkness that inhabits this camp to leave at once. We ban you from ever returning here."

The wind and thunder subsided. Tatyana glanced up. The dark clouds covering the camp withdrew, allowing her to see the starlit sky.

"No!" screamed Mueller.

Tatyana released Maja's hand. "Thank you."

"My pleasure." Maja went back to strengthening the outer circle.

Mueller crouched down, his face inches from Maja. "Bitch, you'll pay for this."

Maja poured more salt into the circle and smiled. "Come and get me."

Tatyana stepped over and placed a hand on the monolith. An intense aura immediately surrounded her. Not the pain and suffering of earlier, but one of pleasure and excitement. She placed her other hand on the monolith, lowered her head, and closed her eyes. This time, she spoke in a soft, gentle voice.

"You're no longer trapped. The darkness that held you

here is gone. The SS no longer have control over you. You're free. Move on to your afterlife and leave your pain and suffering behind you."

Tatyana sensed a massive feeling of gratitude. Then the aura drained away like water behind a burst dam. The spectral image of Cyna appeared before Tatyana in a semi-corporeal form. She stretched out her arm. Tatyana reached out, clasping the girl's fingers in her own.

"Thank you," said Cyna, a tear of happiness in her eyes.

The image dissipated. Within seconds, the residual energy flowed from Treblinka.

Nick stared at the sky. "Will you look at that."

Tatyana glanced up. A bright, white aurora streaked the sky above them and pulsated for several seconds before melting away.

Tatyana approached the outer circle of salt, pleased to see that the SS officers were terrified.

"What should we do with them?" asked Maja.

"Let them rot here for all I care," said Nick.

Tatyana shook her head. "This place is now hallowed ground. I refuse to soil it with their presence."

She entered the third circle. Rather than attack her, the three officers backed away. The German Shepperd's tail curled between his legs and he backed away, whimpering. The Alsatian lowered its head and front paws to the ground, recognizing who was in control. Tatyana crouched in front of them.

"You two had no control over your actions. You were trained to be cruel. I release you from this realm. I'll let the spirit world decide your fate. May you find forgiveness and redemption."

The images of the canines slowly dissolved and scattered into the night sky.

Tatyana stood and faced the SS officers. "You enjoyed the evil you inflicted on these people in life and reveled in the control you possessed over them in death. You showed no mercy and, as such, deserve no mercy."

Mueller stepped forward defiantly. "What do you plan on doing with us?"

Tatyana did not answer. Instead, she stepped outside the circle, her gaze focused on the three perpetrators of evil.

"I refuse to show fear and back down from the darkness. I banish hate and anger from my own life. As shall it be with me, shall it be with this location. Purest entities of the spiritual world, grant me the strength to banish these entities. Help me to thrust into Hell the vile spirits that dwell in the remains of this camp and all who thrive off the misery and suffering of those who are good and righteous. I cast these blights on humanity back to the realm of evil where they belong. May they forever suffer in the pits of darkness."

A rumbling shook the ground. Flames rose from the dirt, engulfing the SS officers. Their spiritual forms burst into flames. If they had been corporeal, their agony would have been unimaginable yet well deserved. Mueller raised his right arm in a Nazi salute, a final act of defiance before the spectral images were incinerated. The flames puffed out, leaving a smoldering pile of black ash where they had stood only moments before.

An awkward silence followed.

Stanisław spoke first. "Is that it?"

"Yes. We succeeded."

Beata seemed hopeful. "There are no more spirits here?"

"None."

Maja closed her eyes. "There's a spiritual serenity to this place that hasn't been felt since before the camp was built."

Beata hugged Tatyana, then Maja. "Thank you. Thank you both."

"My pleasure."

"I wouldn't use the word pleasure," teased Maja. "But after tonight, any other paranormal experiences I have will pale in comparison."

"You did good." Nick stepped up to Tatyana. "Honestly, I didn't think we'd win this one."

"Oh, ye of little faith." Tatyana chuckled. "How's your arm and leg?"

"They'd be in bad shape if I had a body."

"Are you talking to your ghost friend?" asked Stanisław.

"Yes."

"Thank him for his help."

"I will."

"What now?" asked Beata.

"You and Stanisław wait here. Maja and I are going to a final cleansing of the camp to make sure no evil spirits remain and none can return, then we'll head home."

CHAPTER TWENTY-ONE

TATYANA PACKED THE suitcase and travel bag that sat open on the bed. Nostradamus watched from his perch on top of the pillows, occasionally getting an ear scratch. Once sure she had gathered all her belongings, she closed the suitcase, zipped up the bag, and placed her passport and airline tickets beside them. Checking her watch, she had fifteen minutes before the driver arrived to take her to the airport.

Nick materialized beside Tatyana, causing her to jump. She punched his arm, knowing the fist would not touch him.

"Will you stop doing that? You know it scares me."

"It keeps your guard up." Nostradamus barked once. Nick motioned to the dog. "See, even he agrees."

"He doesn't know any better."

Nick stepped over and petted Nostradamus. "Your mistress likes to complain."

"You must have been the most aggravating of your siblings."

"I was the middle child, with an older brother and a younger sister. Aggravation was how I attracted attention."

"Figures," Tatyana mumbled, a smile on her lips.

"I bet you won't miss this place."

"I won't miss Treblinka, but I would love to come back someday and see more of Poland. It's a beautiful country—not what I expected."

Nick scratched behind Nostradamus' ear. "What did you expect?"

"I don't know. A run-down Communist society?"

"That was thirty years ago. Eastern Europe has bounced back since those days."

Tatyana nodded. Thankfully, the forces of evil could not withstand positive energy when used correctly.

"What can I do for you?"

"I'm just here to wish you a safe trip."

"You're not going to stay with me on the plane and bother me on the flight back?"

"You'd watch romantic comedies. No, thanks. I'll meet you when you get home."

"I'm sure you'll be there to bother me," she teased.

"Nah. I'll give you a day to relax before I pester you." Nick paused. "You did good at the camp."

"Thanks. However, I should have listened to you. I was in way over my head with a two-ton anchor tied around my feet."

"If you had, those spirits would still be trapped at Treblinka, suffering endless torment by the SS. You freed them. My problem was my lack of faith in you. I didn't think you could handle something so intense."

"Nick Thompson admits he's wrong? I must have died during the cleansing and gone to heaven."

"Joke all you want. The fact is, I underestimated you, and that was wrong of me. By now, I should realize you can handle anything the spirit world throws at you." Nick paused again. "I want to apologize for that."

"Accepted." Tayana smiled. "I'll see you in a few days."

"You can count on it."

Nick dematerialized and disappeared with his usual loud pop. Nostradamus barked once, missing his friend. This time, Tatyana did not get aggravated at Nick's exit.

Someone knocked on the door. Tatyana answered it, surprised to find Stanisław standing there along with Piotr.

"Come in."

"Thanks." Stanisław stepped inside. "Where's your luggage?"

"In the bedroom."

Stanisław spoke to the driver in Polish. He nodded, entered the bedroom, and left with the suitcase and travel bag a minute later.

"I didn't expect to see you here."

"I wanted to thank you again personally for everything you did and to give you this." Stanisław pulled an envelope from his inner jacket pocket. "Here are your airline tickets."

"Thanks, but I already have them."

"Not these. My office upgraded you to a private jet. It's the least we could do."

The gesture caught Tatyana by surprise. She took the tickets and examined them. "Thank you."

"My pleasure. In all my years with the CBSP. I've never experienced anything like the other day, and I seriously doubt I ever will again."

"You'll have some great stories to tell your grandchildren."

"I don't think they'll believe me." Stanisław chuckled. "I also wanted to tell you that Maja and Danuta visited the camp yesterday. They said the place is cleansed of all spirits. Even Beata feels a serenity about the place she hasn't before. Danuta asked me to give you this."

He reached into his pocket again and pulled out a small, oblong box, which he handed to Tatyana. She opened it. A gold pendant rested on the red velvet interior. The attached gold pendant was comprised of the words NEVER AGAIN.

"That's so sweet."

"Danuta said you deserved it, considering what you did for those spirits at Treblinka. She also blessed it with sage and sea salt to help ward off any evil attached to you."

Tatyana removed the necklace and, with Stanisław's help, placed it around her neck. When finished, she hugged Stanisław.

"What's that for?"

"For everything you did. I wouldn't have succeeded without you, Nick, and the women."

"You're welcome. The car is ready when you are."

"I want to take Nostradamus for a quick walk first."

"I'll do that."

Tatyana called Nostradamus, who bounded off the bed and raced into the suite. She placed the harness around his chest and handed the leash to Stanisław. "You be a good boy. I'll join you in a minute."

"Take your time. The plane won't leave until you get there."

Stanisław led Nostradamus down the hall, the latter's tail wagging.

Tatyana took her jacket off the bed, slipped it on, and slid the passport and plane tickets into the inside pocket. She paused at the door and took a final look at the suite.

She had come a long way since first realizing she could speak with the spirit world. If someone had told her after she freed Nick and the others from the mansion in Eden Hollow that one day she would be cleansing close to a million souls from a death camp and battling the SS, she would have called them crazy. Insane better described all the spiritual encounters she had gone through these past two years. Though Tatyana never told anyone, not even Nick, she had decided to write her memoirs. People needed to be made aware of the evil that existed in the spiritual realm. Who knows, it might inspire others with the same gift to engage in paranormal activity.

Exiting the suite, Tatyana closed the door and headed down the hall. It took the elevator only a few seconds to arrive. She stepped on and pressed the button for the lobby.

Though she would write her memoirs, Tatyana knew she would never give up performing supernatural investigations. It was too rewarding to set free spirits trapped in this realm against their will. The gift she possessed was a calling, one she could not ignore. As bad as Salem, the *Maria Dorea*, and Bethlehem Asylum were, they paled in comparison to her latest cleansing. Tatyana seriously doubted she would ever again encounter anything so frightening.

The elevator doors opened, and Tatyana stepped out. As she made her way across the lobby, she recalled what her grandmother always said about being overconfident.

Never say never.

Preview of *A WORLD GONE DARK: RAVAGED SKIES*

12 July 2024

NOTHING SMELLS BETTER than the aroma of bacon sizzling in the frying pan.

Except for freshly brewed Dunkin' Donuts coffee.

Danielle Costner stood in front of the oven cooking the family's traditional Friday morning breakfast: scrambled eggs, bacon, home fries, and dark rye toast. They started every Friday with a good breakfast and ended it gathered around the big-screen TV in the living room watching a double feature. Shawn got to pick tonight, and her brother had chosen *Oppenheimer* and *Godzilla Minus One*, saying the two were related, though she could not figure out how.

As the food cooked, Danielle used the remote to turn on the TV mounted on the wall across from the counter. She hated the usual morning line-up. It was mostly biased newscasts or even more biased talk shows. She kept it on WMUR to watch the local news, partly to discover what was happening in southern New Hampshire, but mainly for the traffic update. Her morning commute took her into downtown Boston, and Danielle wanted to prepare herself for whatever circle of Hell the traffic would be like today.

The chief meteorologist was on.

"…can expect it to happen anytime between later this afternoon through Saturday evening. Back to you, Jess."

"I thought solar flares were dangerous?" asked Jessica Waters, the morning co-anchor.

"Only the big ones are."

"But you just said this was the largest flare ever recorded by NASA."

"It is, but you have to consider the size of the flare, which is small compared to the solar system. The odds of it hitting Earth are greater than winning Mega Millions."

"Which is the perfect segue to our next story." David Perrine, the other co-anchor, steered the conversation back on track. "Tuesday night's winner of the three hundred and fifty-six million Mega Millions jackpot is a local citizen from Laconia. Margaret—"

Danielle hit the mute button. She was not the winner, so she did not care. Maybe someday she would hit it big, then she could move out of her brother's house and get her own place. Not that she had anything to complain about. Shawn owned a luxurious two-family house in Dunbarton. He lived in the smaller twin-bedroom portion and let Danielle and her daughter live rent-free in the main house. The only downside was the property was pristine, so Shawn would not let them have a dog, and she desperately wanted one.

A door opened upstairs, followed by the blaring of obnoxiously loud music. Kirstie, her sixteen-year-old, came down the stairs sounding like a herd of buffalo. As she entered the kitchen, Kirstie dropped her coat, backpack, and computer bag on the floor before sitting at the counter.

Danielle was proud of her daughter. Kirstie did not have the best grades, all Cs with one B in Social Studies, but she was a good girl who did not do drugs, drink, or get knocked up like so many of the others in her sophomore class. Probably because the girl lived on her cellphone. Kirstie was two inches taller than her mother and had a lean body that was maturing rapidly. Soon, she would have to deal with her little girl dating. However, that might take a while. Kirstie wore combat boots, expensive jeans shredded at the knees, and a sweatshirt with a band logo she had never heard of. Her daughter had naturally brunette hair, like her mother, but with streaks of blue and pink on one side. Someday, Danielle would have to teach Kirstie how to use a comb.

"No electronics at the table."

"What?" Kirstie yelled over the music.

Danielle took the phone from her and turned off the music. "You know I don't like you playing with your cellphone while we eat."

Kirstie huffed as if her life was over.

Danielle placed a plate in front of her daughter. "What do you want to drink?"

"Coffee." Kirstie stared at her mother. "Are you going to wear that to work?"

"Wear what?"

"Uncle's old denim shirt."

"No way." Danielle opened the shirt to reveal her red dress underneath and black heels. "I'm wearing this so I don't get grease splattered on me."

"Whatever."

Danielle poured a cup of coffee and placed it on the counter. "So, are we ready for movie night?"

"About that." Kirstie averted her gaze. "The girls and I are going to Canobie Lake tonight for the grand opening of their new Ferris Wheel."

"Can't you go tomorrow?"

"Ellen and Michelle have to work tomorrow."

At least they have jobs, thought Danielle. "You know we always reserve Friday night for the family."

"But they're debuting their new Ferris Wheel today. Half off all tickets."

"I don't ask much of you."

Kirstie laughed.

"I don't. I just want us to spend time together before you go to college."

"If I go to college."

Danielle's eyes widened. "What do you mean if?"

"What? Wrack up a huge student loan debt to get a job at Shaw's? I'm thinking of going to trade—"

The back door opened, and Shawn stepped in, cutting off the argument. Though twelve years older than her, he still looked in his late thirties. Of average height, with piercing blue eyes and a charming smile, Danielle could not understand why he did not have a steady girlfriend. Actually, she did understand. Shawn was devoted to his job as a shift supervisor at Seabrook Nuclear Power Plant. He always said that with his good looks and his good job, he could have any woman he pleased, to which she always joked that he never pleased any of them.

"Good morning, ladies. Breakfast smells good."

"Thanks." Danielle hugged her brother. "Want some?"

"I can't. Bob called in sick. His wife went into labor early. I'm taking over his shift."

"So that means you'll be missing movie night?"

"Sorry, sis."

Kirstie perked up. "You can't be mad at me if I miss it, too."

Shawn glanced over at his niece. "You won't be here?"

"She wants to go to Canobie Lake with her friends."

He smiled. "You girls want to be there for the opening of the new Ferris Wheel."

"See. Uncle understands."

Shawn turned to his sister and flashed her pouty eyes. "We'll postpone movie night until tomorrow. I'll get Chinese food to make it special. What do you say?"

"I know when I'm outnumbered. Do you want a cup of coffee to go?"

"No, thanks. I prefer my coffee iced. I'll stop by Dunkin' on the way to work." Then to Kirstie, "Do you want a ride?"

"No, thanks. Regan is picking me up. We're going to play video games at her house until Ellen and Michelle join us later."

As if on cue, a horn blared from the driveway.

"There she is." Kirstie jumped off the bar stool and headed for her pile of personal belongings.

"What about your breakfast?"

The teenager ran back, placed the three strips of bacon between her teeth, grabbed her stuff, and headed for the front door.

"Aren't you even going to say goodbye?"

Kirstie waved without looking back and left, slamming the door behind her.

Danielle shook her head. "You're lucky you don't have kids."

"I consider Kirstie my own kid. I just don't have to deal with all the bullshit."

Shawn left out the back door.

Danielle sighed. She made breakfast for three, and now she had leftovers. If she had a dog, she could give it to him. Screw it. She would reheat the meal tonight for supper.

Putting the food on a plate, she placed it in the fridge and moved the dirty dishes and frying pan into the sink. She would worry about cleaning later. Right now, she had to head out for work before the traffic became too horrendous.

Acknowledgments

I spent months contemplating whether or not to write this novel considering the subject matter, eventually deciding that the story of the Holocaust needed to be told since the nightmare is rapidly being forgotten. In light of the recent rise of anti-Semitism over the past several months, I'm glad I did. The story of the suffering of those who were exterminated merely for being Jewish needs to be told.

As many of you know, I am a historian with a particular interest in World War II and the Cold War. Back in 2016, my second wife, Alison, and I visited Treblinka. She can detect the presence of those in the spiritual realm and, as such, found this particular experience extremely disturbing. When she reached the monolith, where the gas chambers were located, Alison could not breathe and had to move away from the site. After that, she spent the entire time being contacted by the souls of those slaughtered there. That became the basis for this novel.

I conducted considerable research on Treblinka to ensure I accurately related the facts about the establishment of this death camp and what happened to those condemned to walk through its gates. Most of my research was from Chil Rajchman's *Treblinka: A Survivor's Memory*. None of the incidents in the flashback chapter have been fictionalized or dramatized. This is what those who arrived at Treblinka endured.

Many thanks go out to my beta readers, Doc Fried and Dungeon Dan Uebel, who have been with me for years. They point out grammatical/spelling errors and inconsistencies and offer their opinion on whether they like the story. In this case, they provided insights that helped me to make this novel more accurate and compelling. I would be lost without them. Like all my others, this book is a much better read because of them.

As they do with my other Tatyana books, Warren Design created the cover for *The Ghosts of Treblinka* based on photographs taken during my visit there. Their work on this particular cover is outstanding.

I recently started a full-time job as a teacher at a charter academy in Manchester, which severely restraints my time to write. It also means that when I get home, my pets are so happy to see me they want to dominate my time. Fred, AKA Turd Burglar, my stubborn Beagle-Bassett mix, is always with me when I write, and sometimes I spend more time keeping him out of trouble than I do at my computer. My cat Archer has discovered that my plugged-in laptop makes the perfect heating pad, so getting him to move is next to impossible. At night, while editing and managing social media, my other cat, Michonne, stands in front of my desktop computer, demanding attention. They make the writing process difficult, but it doesn't matter. I love them all.

The biggest thanks go to my readers, especially those who have been with me from the beginning. Writing is the fun part of my job. I appreciate all of you who read my books and patiently wait for the next one. I have a lot of stories floating around inside my head, and I am looking forward to sharing them with you.

About the Author

Scott M. Baker was born and raised in Everett, Massachusetts, and spent twenty-three years in northern Virginia working for the Central Intelligence Agency. He has traveled extensively through Europe, Asia, and the Middle East, incorporating many of the locations and cultures in his stories. Scott is now retired and lives outside Salem, New Hampshire, with his dog Fred and two cats who treat him as their human servant.

Scott is currently writing *The Chronicles of Paul* saga, his latest zombie apocalypse series; his Tatyana paranormal series; and his soon-to-be-released *A World Gone Dark* novel that will tell the story of a handful of survivors of a massive solar event and how they deal with a world deprived of electricity. Previous works include the *Nurse Alissa vs. the Zombies* series, his most popular zombie saga; *Operation Majestic*, his first science fiction novel described as *Raiders of the Lost Ark* meets *Back to the Future* – with aliens; *Frozen World*, his first non-zombie post-apocalypse novel; the *Shattered World* series, his five-book young adult post-apocalypse thriller; *The Vampire Hunters* trilogy, about humans fighting the undead in Washington D.C.; *Yeitso*, his homage to the giant monster movies of the 1950s that he loved watching as a kid; as well as several zombie-themed novellas and anthologies.

Facebook:
facebook.com/groups/397749347486177

Twitter:
twitter.com/vampire_hunters

Instagram:
instagram.com/scottmbakerwriter

Blog:
scottmbakerauthor.blogspot.com

YouTube:
youtube.com/channel/UC5AyCVrEAncr2E0N5XoyUdg/feat
ured

Wyrd Realities Homepage:
www.wyrdrealities.net

You can also sign up for Scott's newsletter, which will be released on the 1st and 15th of every month. He promises not to share your email with anyone or spam the recipients. The newsletter contains advance notices of upcoming releases/events and short stories from the Alissa, Paul, and Tatyana universes that will not be available to the public. You can sign up by clicking the link below.

Newsletter:
mailchi.mp/0b1401f1ddb2/scott-m-baker-writer